D1563009

Gentleman

James

and

Gina

MALLORY MONROE

AUSTIN BROOK PUBLISHING

**THE RAGS TO ROMANCE SERIES
STANDALONE BOOKS**

IN ORDER:

**1. BOBBY SINATRA: IN ALL THE WRONG
PLACES**

2. BOONE & CHARLY: SECOND CHANCE LOVE

3. PLAIN JANE EVANS AND THE BILLIONAIRE

4. GENTLEMAN JAMES AND GINA

MALLORY MONROE SERIES:

**THE RENO GABRINI/MOB BOSS SERIES (20
BOOKS)**

THE SAL GABRINI SERIES (12 BOOKS)

THE TOMMY GABRINI SERIES (9 BOOKS)

THE MICK SINATRA SERIES (13 BOOKS)

THE BIG DADDY SINATRA SERIES (7 BOOKS)

THE TEDDY SINATRA SERIES (4 BOOKS)

THE TREVOR REESE SERIES (3 BOOKS)

THE AMELIA SINATRA SERIES (2 BOOKS)

THE BRENT SINATRA SERIES (1 BOOK)

THE ALEX DRAKOS SERIES (8 BOOKS)

THE OZ DRAKOS SERIES (2 BOOKS)

THE MONK PALETTI SERIES (2 BOOKS)

THE PRESIDENT'S GIRLFRIEND SERIES (8 BOOKS)

THE PRESIDENT'S BOYFRIEND SERIES (1 BOOK)

ALSO

AUSTIN BROOK PUBLISHING

STANDALONE BOOKS:

ROMANCING MO RYAN

MAEBELLE MARIE

LOVING HER SOUL MATE

LOVING THE HEAD MAN

VISIT
www.mallorymonroebooks.com

OR

www.austinbrookpublishing.com

for more information on all titles.

TABLE OF CONTENTS

GENTLEMAN JAMES AND GINA

PROLOGUE

Fifteen Years Earlier

"Ah, come on, GG. It'll be fun!"

But Gina Griffin knew her idea of fun and Kim McCoy's idea were two different things. She continued to clean off the table in the crowded sports bar, as her close friend sat at a nearby table. Begging her. "It'll be fun," Kim said again.

"The idea of going to some frat party when we have midterms makes no sense, Kimmie," Gina said. "We need to take every moment we have to be studying."

"Girl please! Those exams are a week away. We'll ace those stupid tests easily."

But Gina shook her head and continued cleaning. "*You'll* ace those exams. I'll study my butt off and be lucky if I get a B."

Kim laughed. "I told you to cheat like the rest of us."

"No thanks."

"But why not, G? Those professors look the other way because they need us to do well so they can brag to rich parents about their success rate. They want us to cheat."

"Even if that were true, it'll still be wrong."

Kim rolled her eyes. "Just come with me, Gina, please. We're missing all the fun!"

"I'm working anyway. Remember that little fact? I can't just leave."

"How much are they paying you an hour?"

Gina looked at Kim. "What does that have to do with anything?"

"How much?"

Gina exhaled. "Two-fifty plus tips."

"And how much longer do you have to work?"

"I have another hour left."

"Then I'll give you twenty bucks and you can call it a day," Kim declared. "And then you can go to the party with me!"

Gina couldn't help but smile and shake her head at her friend's tenacity. "It doesn't work like that, Kimmie."

"Why doesn't it? I'll be paying you way more than you'll make in the next hour. Why can't you just do it?"

"Because I have a responsibility to work

until my shift is over. That's what I signed up for."

"Ah, GG, stop being such a party pooper and come on."

"You can go," Gina said. "Go 'head on. I'm not stopping you. You don't need me there too."

"Yes, I do," Kim said with defeat in her voice. "They won't let me in unless I have a hot girl with me."

It was Gina's time to roll her eyes. She never liked when anybody referred to her as hot or great looking or any of those descriptors. She felt they were grossly overstating it, for one thing, and being so-called *hot* got her in nothing but hot water when she was a kid and had to deal with grown men leering at her and their wives claiming it was her fault for being pretty. Or boys doing all they could to get inside her panties when all she wanted was to be left alone. And when she became a teenager and a few times gave in to the attention, it turned out disastrous. Kim could say whatever she liked, but Gina never equated being hot with anything but trouble.

"If I don't have a hot girl with me, they'll turn me away at the gate," Kim said, ignoring Gina's eye roll. "You know how they are at those parties. No hot girl, no entry. I need a hot girl!"

"Then you'd better go find one," said Gina.

Kim always found Gina's lack of self-awareness offensive when she would give her right arm to look that great. "I'm looking at one," she said. "And you know it."

Gina frowned. "I know no such thing. Don't put that on me."

"Gina, just come on! I want to meet some boys and have some fun. What's wrong with that? The guy at the gate won't let me in if I don't have a hot girl with me."

Gina stopped and looked at Kim. "Do you listen to yourself sometimes?" she asked her.

"What?"

"They won't let you in unless you have somebody hot with you," Gina said.

"Yeah, so?"

"So? Kim! Why would you want to go to a party like that?"

"That's how they operate," said Kim. "I don't make the rules. I just want to be a part of it."

"But why would you want to be a part of something that doesn't want you there on your own merits?"

"Because that's how it is, Gina, okay?

That's how it is! Now are you going with me or not? They won't let me in if you don't go with me."

"What makes you so certain of that?" Gina asked her.

Kim looked away from her. "Because I tried already," she said.

Gina stopped cleaning off the table and looked at her friend. She so wanted to be accepted in that world of frat parties and frat boys when Gina knew neither one of them would ever be fully accepted in that world. They were two black girls in a town that was ninety-nine percent white, attending a college that was ninety-eight percent non-black. For Gina, it was *get the degree and go*. For Kim, it was *let's mingle*! Kim, it went without saying, was having the harder time.

"Say yes, GG," Kim pleaded. "We're freshmen. We've never been to a frat party yet, and this one is a good first try because it isn't at a frat house. It's a pool party, which means it'll be cleaner and even more fun. It's a part of college life. Please don't let me have to go alone and get rejected again."

"But who's to say you won't get rejected once you get in the party, Kim?"

"Because I'll have my personality and quick wit to sustain me," Kim said with her beautiful, ready smile. "Not to mention Daddy's money to throw around. I just want to have some fun for a change."

Gina looked at her friend. They were so different that it surprised her how they were friends at all. Gina was from a working-class family and was considered universally beautiful. Kim was from a rich family and was considered universally fun and vibrant, but quite plain. Gina worked hard for everything she earned, including the scholarship she won to Bayard, the private liberal arts college they attended in upstate New York. But Kim was cheating her way through school like many of the rich white kids they went to school with. She, like them, had no hesitancy with paying others to let her cheat on their papers, rightly knowing that some professors looked the other way. But that was Bayard. The faculty, like the booster clubs and alumni association, just wanted to hand out great grades to boast about to other rich kids looking to attend the august body. They just wanted to be able to put in a slick flyer that ninety-nine percent of their students maintained a high A average, or some other ridiculously untrue metric.

"Do it for me, Gina," said Kim. "You know if the shoe was on the other foot, I'd do it for you."

Gina knew no such thing. But she saw the desperation in Kim's eyes. She truly thought attending some nothing frat party was going to be a life-changing event.

"You said it was a pool party and we don't even have bathing suits, Kimmie," Gina said, trying to find even more reasons to avoid going.

Kim reached into her bag and pulled out two brand new bikinis. "I already bought them," she said. "One for me, and one for you. Brand new so you can't complain. Just say yes, please."

Gina exhaled. "Okay, I'll go," she said that fateful night, and Kim jumped up and hugged her neck. "But only after I finish my shift," Gina added.

Kim stopped embracing her. "I told you I'll pay you to leave now," she said. But before Gina could scold her about what's right and ethical and all of that, she smiled. "But I'll take it. I'll wait until you clock off. Thanks, Genevieve!"

When Kim called Gina by her real name, she gave Kim that *no you didn't* look that made Kim laugh again.

But then Gina got serious. "If it starts getting crazy at this party," she said, "we're leaving. Okay, Kim? I'm out. With or without you."

Kim nodded vigorously. She would have promised her anything. "Absolutely," she said.

"No," the man at the gate said to a couple of plain-looking white girls who tried to get into the back yard where the party sounded as if it was already in full swing. The girls left embarrassed and Gina wondered who in their right mind would subject themselves to such harshness.

Kim McCoy, that was who, she thought, when Kim stepped up to the gate with that great smile on her face.

But the guy at the gate wasn't buying it. "No," the big, burly, bouncer-type said to Kim, too, and by rights they should have turned themselves around and left like the white girls did. But not Kim McCoy. She thrust Gina in front of her! "I'm with her," she said.

The bouncer didn't have to look Gina up and down for long. Just one good glance and he approved her, as if she was exactly the look they wanted at that party. He quickly let Gina, with Kim, right on in.

"Told you," Kim said as they entered the gate that led to the pool party around back. But her smile was gone. Gina could tell it was still humiliating for Kim.

"I still say you shouldn't want this," said

Gina.

"Well, I've got it now," Kim said, her smile returning, her arm in Gina's arm. "And guess what? You've got it too!"

"Bathing suits ten dollars!" a vendor was calling out. "Bathing suits ten dollars!"

"Come on," Kim said, pulling Gina along. "Let's go get changed!"

Gina realized she was there, now, and might as well enjoy the pool if nothing else. "Why not?" she said, and Kim, happy to have her onboard finally, all but dragged her into one of the guest houses where they changed quickly, and then decided to race each other to the pool. They both jumped in happily, as the other kids were doing, and Gina was actually enjoying herself. Until the boys wouldn't quit.

One after the other one kept trying to hit on Gina. She knew what they wanted, and she wasn't having it, but turning them down was taking all the fun out of even being in the pool. So she eventually got out, found herself an empty lounger, and decided to get on it, lean back, and people watch.

Kim was still in the pool having a blast, Gina could see, and a couple guys were talking to her. Although both of them seemed more interested in her body than in her conversation, but wasn't that the whole point to a party like that? Invite the girls over and see how far they'd let you go? And soon enough, Kim was out of the pool and smiling and waving at Gina as some boy was escorting her toward the main house. To one of the bedrooms no doubt.

But Gina believed in the adage that you didn't let your girl go it alone at any party. That you kept an eye on your girl no matter what. And Gina got up and hurried over to Kim.

"Kimmie, can I talk to you for a minute?" she asked her.

Kim didn't like the interruption, it was clear on her face, but she told the boy to hang on a sec. And she and Gina moved away from his earshot.

"Don't do it, Kim," said Gina. "That boy's got nothing but sex on his mind."

"And what you think I got on my mind?" asked Kim. "Exams?"

Gina stared at her. "Desperation will make a fool out of you every time, girl. You'll regret it in the morning."

A sad look appeared in Kim's eyes, but then she rallied as she always did. And she smiled. "If you aren't regretting, you aren't living," she said, and went on over to the frat boy who gladly led her upstairs.

Gina felt bad for her friend, but what could she do? Kim was a big girl with a lot of big girl experience. Way more than Gina ever had, and Gina had had her share of bad boys already herself. She'd had her full of them, in fact. Kim wanted to do her thing, and Gina had to let her. She went back to the lounger, and she reclined again.

And she continued to people watch. Which, she had to admit, was kind of enjoyable in its own way too. Mainly because there were some funny cast of characters at that party, and they were making her laugh at their little hijinks.

But as she continued to look around, she saw one particular guy on the opposite side of the pool. He, like her, was leaned back on a lounger too. But unlike her, he wasn't people watching at all. He seemed to have his eyes closed, as if he were bored to tears.

What surprised her about him was the fact that he seemed so much older than the boys and girls at the party. And she wasn't talking a few years older either. He looked like, if he had ever attended Bayard at all, he attended it years ago. Nearly a decade ago she'd say. She was eighteen. He could easily be in his upper twenties. Which begged the question to Gina: why on earth would he want to be at some bad boy frat party?

And he had that grown look too. Black, curly hair like Dean Martin's. A smoking body as his shirtless chest and six-pack abs revealed just how well-built he was. Wearing nothing but a pair of trunks, he was nicely packed, too, with what appeared to be an extra-large package midway down. He looked like a man among boys to Gina in every way. And if her belief about his age was right, that was exactly what he was: a man among boys. And a very good-looking man at that!

But then what appeared to be a very good-looking younger man, a boy around Gina's age, walked up and sat on the edge of the lounger with him. And then he got all the way on the lounger and sat shoulder to shoulder with the older man the way a couple would do. And based on the way the guy woke up and was interacting with the kid, Gina made a snap decision. He's gay, she decided, as she watched the two men interact. Why else would he let some guy sit beside him on a lounger the way you would let your woman sit there? That was why he wasn't running after any of those girls at the party either. He wanted the boys! Which made her smile. The only guy that caught her attention at that whole party was gay. That was how her luck was running. That was why she always picked the wrong one. She was losing her touch, she thought jokingly, if she ever had any touch at all.

And her eyes moved on. No point in salivating over something she knew she could not have. She kept on looking, and checking people out, and laughing at the silliness. Until she became so relaxed that she fell asleep.

But across the pool, unbeknownst to Gina, the man she thought was gay wasn't trying to pick up the young man who had sat on the lounger beside him. He was scolding the young man, because the young man was his baby brother.

"He told you a few of your closest friends, Vinny," James Serrano said to the younger man. "Just a few of your closest friends. But this is a fucking *y'all come*!"

"How was I to control how many people showed up? I thought it would just be a few of my friends."

"Sure you did, Vinny. And I'm dumb too."

Vincent Serrano laughed. "You might be! Besides, everybody's having such fun. I don't see what's the problem, or why he figured you had to be here at all."

"There's a threat out there, and he wanted to make sure I kept an eye on the situation. He's looking out for you."

"But I don't need looking out for. I can take care of myself."

"Sure buddy," said James. "Just like you

almost got yourself killed sleeping with that man's wife and I had to get you out of that little situation too."

But Vincent was mortified. "You told Carmine?" he asked anxiously. "Is that why he made you come this time? Please tell me you didn't tell Carmine, Jimmy."

"No, I didn't tell him. What do you take me for? If I would have told him, he would have hauled your ass back to Chicago by now. No, I didn't tell him."

Vincent relaxed again.

"But I am going to tell him about this free-for-all when he told you to keep it small. Our big brother is paying for this place for you. And he told you he didn't want his house to become a frat house. Which is exactly what you turned it into. Look at this wild crowd. And you can take care of yourself? Yeah, right!"

"Don't you have a law practice to run?" Vincent asked his older brother. "Don't you have a life of your own to lead on a Friday night?"

James looked at Vincent. "I hate babysitting your ass as much as you hate being babysat. Just make sure you stay within the borders of this house and my job will have been successful. All of these people running around everywhere? You'd better handle that."

Vincent looked at James. "But you aren't gonna tell him how many people showed up, right?"

"Am I going to tell him that the house he purchased for you to have a comfortable place to live while you got your education at Bayard is being trashed as we speak?"

"Yeah. You won't tell him, right?"

James shook his head. "You're hopeless, Vinny."

"Just don't tell him, okay? About the crowd I mean. About the drinking. About none of it. Okay, Jimmy? I don't wanna hear his mouth. You know how he is."

"Okay already! Now just leave me alone."

"With pleasure," Vincent said with a smile and kissed his brother on the cheek. "I've got a girl waiting upstairs for me anyway."

"What girl? Penny?"

"Hell naw! She gets on my nerves."

"What she's done now?"

"She's always pronouncing our name wrong. I tell her over and over it's Serrano. *Sir* like sir. *Rah* like rah-rah, let's cheer somebody. And then no. *Sir-rah-no*. But her ass always pronouncing it Sur-*ran*-no. I tell her quit with the ran, why do you keep saying ran? It's *Ser-rah-no*. Not *Ser-ran-no*. But she says that's how it's spelled: Ser-ran-no. I got tired of that."

James shook his head. "You immature little boy."

"Whatever!"

"So, she's not here then?"

"No. I didn't tell her about it. But anyway, I'm out," Vincent said, getting off of the lounger. "I've got business upstairs. I'll talk to you later," he added, and then hurried away.

James shook his head again. Vinny was a party boy through and through and that was all he'd ever be. Why Carmine was wasting his money trying to give him an education was a mystery to James. But there it was. Vinny was a freshman in college, paying a guy to pretend to be him and to go to class for him, while James, who actually benefited from a world-class education, was in his fourth year as a practicing attorney. But he and Vincent were like night and day. Although Vincent was right about one thing: James did have better things to do with his Friday nights than traveling to Latham to babysit a baby like Vincent.

And just as he tried to close his eyes again, to at least get some much-needed rest, another young woman came up to his lounger attempting to interest him in her and her beauty. But he wasn't interested and made it clear by his disinterested look alone. She, like the other women at that get together, weren't just too young for him, but they were so immature that it astounded him.   He wasn't interested in the least.

And for several more minutes he remained uninterested. Until he looked across the pool, and saw her lounging there.

She was one of only a handful of black girls at the entire party, and even from where he sat, he could tell she had that smoking-hot, sleek black body that always turned him on ever since he was a little boy staring at African women in those National Geographic magazines. But she was beginning to worry him.

Mainly because it appeared as if she might have been knocked out drunk, which was a bad idea at a party like that one. She was just lying there, with her eyes closed, and he could see various boys taking peeps at her. But then a pattern started emerging. He noticed that every time some young guy would approach her lounger, she would open her eyes as if she could smell him coming. Then she'd turn him down with one of those *don't even try it* looks that made no apologies, he'd leave her alone, and then she'd doze right back off like clockwork. James smiled. She was precise if she was anything, he thought.

And it happened again. And then again. She'd wake up just as some guy was approaching her, she'd turn him down, and then she'd doze off again. James was actually enjoying watching her. She was turning out to be the only interesting person at the whole event.

But when one guy made it up to her and actually managed to cop-a-feel on her thigh before she woke up and turned him down, without realizing what he'd done, James had a sudden urge to get over there before one of those testosterone-crazed young men decided to cop more than a thigh feel at her expense. As she dozed back off, he got up and walked over there, staring at her the entire time.

She still hadn't opened her eyes as James approached her the way she had been doing most of the night, mainly because James knew how to approach without detection. But it gave him a chance to get an up close and more personal look at her.

She looked like she was around Vincent's age, which would put her as an eighteen-year-old Freshman, but she had a very well-endowed body with all the right curves a man could crave. And her dark skin looked so soft and velvety that he wanted to reach out and touch it. And her big, natural, curly hair. Just a gorgeous girl! And when she opened her big, dark-green eyes, he was amazed at just how innocent she appeared!

Gina was startled, too, when she realized that the man she had noticed from across the pool, the older gay guy, was now standing at the foot of her chair. She looked at him. He was staring at her. But somehow, Gina thought, it didn't feel creepy.

James Serrano had never been at a loss for words in his entire life. His brother Carmine wanted him to become a lawyer because he had the gift of gab. He was a serial talker. But when Gina opened those eyes, he froze. Momentarily he froze. How could she be so alluring, he wondered, but yet so young?

What shocked Gina was how she wasn't so quick to turn him away the way she'd so easily turned away those other boys at the party. Maybe because he wasn't some immature kid. Maybe because he was so big and powerful-looking compared to everybody else. And his eyes didn't look desperate for sex the way those boys' eyes looked. They just looked kind.

Or maybe it was just because he was gay. Or at least, she realized, she thought he was! Because up close, she didn't see it.

But why would a man who appeared to be in his upper twenties want to be at some frat party with a bunch of college kids? Unless he was a party boy himself, she thought. And that fact quickly put a damper on her interest even more than the fact that he might be gay. "May I help you?" she asked him.

Her words unfroze James. "I saw you lying here from across the pool."

"Yes, I saw you too," Gina said.

"Did you?" James asked. Was she interested in him too?

"I think I dozed off afterwards."

James smiled. "I was so uninteresting that I put you to sleep?"

Gina laughed.

"Is that what you're telling me?" James continued, still smiling too.

"I didn't mean it like that."

"Good. Because that hurts."

Gina continued to smile. "Not my nature to hurt anybody."

"Good," James said again. Then he glanced at the empty lounger beside hers. "Is this seat taken?" he asked her.

"Not to my knowledge," Gina said.

James sat on the edge of the empty lounger, his body turned to her. "The reason I came over," he said, "was because the party put you to sleep."

"It's just not my thing, that's all."

"Then why are you here?"

"My roommate begged me to come. She didn't think they'd let her through the gate unless she had a friend with her."

"You mean a hot friend, right?" James asked.

Gina didn't respond to that. Beauty to her was in the eye of the beholder, and when she looked in the mirror, despite all the compliments she received, she didn't see it.

James, a master at deflection, realized he had touched some nerve. She was one of those good-looking dames who didn't like to be called good looking apparently. His brother Vinny, who was a great looking guy himself, was like that too. "It's nuts though, isn't it? They want a certain look at a party to boost their own fragile egos."

"And that's all it is," said Gina. "I agree with that."

While James had her in agreement with him, he knew he had to press his advantage. She was getting him hard. She could actually give him something to do to beat back his own boredom.

"You don't have to be bored you know," he said, glancing at her body so that she didn't misunderstand him.

Gina saw that he was accessing her.

And she liked the way his eyes roamed over her because it didn't feel dirty to her. It felt as if he just liked what he saw. She didn't respond to his statement, though, until he looked back into her eyes. "I don't?" she asked him.

James saw interest in her eyes too. "No. You most definitely do not. You know why?"

"Why?"

James smiled and opened his arms. "I'm here, baby."

Gina laughed. Was that the line that was supposed to get her in bed? "Is that supposed to reassure me?" she asked him.

"Of course. Doesn't it?"

"Thank you, but no."

James grinned the most charming grin, Gina thought. "Are you serious? It doesn't?"

"Not for a second."

"Damn! I'm losing my touch."

"You're losing something alright," said Gina, and they both laughed.

"But no," James said when the laugher died down, "I was worried about you."

Gina looked doubtful. "Worried about me?"

"When you had fallen asleep. I saw a few boys try to take advantage of you."

Gina was alarmed by that news. "Really?"

"That's what they do at these kinds of parties you know."

Gina nodded. "I know. But I thought I was just closing my eyes."

"And you were. For the most part."

"But a couple creeps got cute anyway?" Gina asked him.

He smiled. "There ya' go."

And James was intrigued by her. He couldn't deny it. He really liked this girl. He didn't like her in any *let's be together forever* kind of way. He wasn't going to go down that road with anybody! But he liked her in a *she's better than anybody else at this free-for-all* kind of way. And he decided to take a chance. He stood up and reached out his hand to her. "Come with me," he said.

Gina found him bold if he was anything. Why on earth would she go anywhere with him? But she wasn't exactly bursting with things to do at that party since Kim had long since deserted her. And she couldn't risk falling asleep again, not after what he told her. And he was older and nice and seemed to have more going on than anybody else at that party. What, she thought, did she have to lose?

Plenty, she would later learn. But she took his hand, anyway, and stood up.

Thirty minutes later, after drinking beer and listening to music in one of the five guest houses that was near the pool area, he moved up against her. And then they were dancing together to the slow-sounding beat. And then they were kissing each other.

Gina had never felt that way before when a boy kissed her, and she suddenly realized this was going to be different. And that *he* was different. And when James began to lift her bikini top as he kissed her, and then moved down and began kissing her bare breasts, Gina also knew that she was in a different ballgame than she was used to playing.

And then he lifted her and carried her to the bed in the room. And Gina, to her own shock, allowed him to do so. And then he began removing his trunks, revealing that thick package she could tell he had from across the pool. And when he removed her bikini panties and got on top of her, she was again shocked when she allowed him to resume kissing her, and her breasts. And when he moved down between her legs, she let him do that too.

She was no virgin, but it had been over a year since she'd been with a boy. But that boy was nothing like this man. Nothing like him! And she found herself in the throes of a kind of heightened passion she had never experienced before.

And when he opened the nightstand drawer, and pulled out a condom, she knew he meant business. This was not going to be a get hot and go home session. He wanted to go all in.

And what would have been unthinkable before she arrived at that party, became a reality. Because when he put on that condom and entered her, she arched and felt his fullness in a way that was almost too big for her to bear. He was too big! But she let him continue. And she was glad she did because his movements were gentle, as he kept easing further in, until she was able to bear it and even enjoy it. Gina was surprised by how much she enjoyed it!

She was also surprised by how quickly she came because she enjoyed it so much. But when she came, it seemed to do something to him, and he began pumping on her so fast and so hard that he began cumming too.

But then she suddenly felt something. And it was liquid. *His* liquid!

He suddenly stopped all movement and looked at her. She had felt so good to James that he had lost all control. And the way she made him cum so quickly! But he realized he'd done it now! "I think it broke," he admitted to her with a frown on his face. "I think my condom broke."

But they were at the apex of cumming. Both of them were. What were they going to do? And when he slowly continued to move inside of her, Gina realized what they were going to do. Because neither one of them could make it stop. Neither one of them wanted it to stop. And when Gina wrapped her arms around him, that move alone gave him the permission he so desperately sought to continue.

And even as they were still cumming, he kept pumping hard. He couldn't stop that either. For several minutes he was cumming and cumming hard and Gina started having rolling orgasms with his cum.

And then he began to slow his roll and was able to have slower and slower movements as their cum finally began to ease.

And when it was over, and they both were breathless and satisfied, he leaned against her, smiling. She remembered that high-wattage smile. She also remembered the arrow tattoo on his big bicep. She rubbed it. "What does the arrow represent?" she asked him.

His smile increased. "You don't miss anything, girl, do you?"

She smiled too. He was a charmer, that was for sure! "What does it represent?" she asked him.

"Direction," James said.

"That's all?"

"That's all."

"Why do you need to remind yourself about direction?"

A sad look appeared in his eyes. "You come from the kind of family I come from," he said, "it's fairly easy to go astray."

Gina didn't know what he meant, but she could tell it was heartfelt. "That's in any family, I think," she said.

He looked at her when she said that, as if she had no clue. "If you only knew," he said to her. But then he smiled, as if he decided not to hold it against her. "You're good, you know that?"

"Good at what?" Gina asked.

"Just good," he said. "Good as gold." Then he added, with that smile again. "And good in bed."

Gina smiled. She knew that was what he meant all along. But just as he was about to say something else to her, a sound suddenly pierced their peace. It was a sound James knew too well, and he jumped out of bed.

"What was that?" Gina was asking him, leaning up. But he had thrown off that broken condom, put on his trunks frantically, and was running toward the exit. He began treating her as she remained: a stranger to him. "Stay in here," he said to her, even as he was running out himself.

And Gina, mortified, hastily jumped out of bed, too, and put back on her bathing suit. Then she hurried to the window to see what was going on. But all she saw were a bunch of kids surrounding another kid who appeared to be lying on the patio near the pool. She thought about Kim, panicked, and hurried outside.

But then Kim came rushing up to her. "Are you alright?" Kim frantically asked Gina, practically running into her.

"I'm fine!" Gina replied just as frantically. "You?"

"I'm fine."

"What happened?" Gina asked.

"I think somebody got shot."

"Who?"

"I don't know who. Just some kid. It's all so unnerving, GG!"

Then Gina saw the man she knew as Ross stand up in that crowd that surrounded the kid on the ground. That was when she saw the kid. He was the same one that had been sitting on the lounger with Ross earlier in the night.

And she was right. Vincent Serrano was on that ground, and he was injured. And James began ordering a group of frat boys to carry him into the main house. He opened the door for them, and they hurried inside Vincent.

Gina was getting scared herself. But then she saw the bouncer that had been at the gate, along with other burly men that looked like bouncers too. The place seemed to suddenly be overrun with various bouncer-looking men. Where did they come from, Gina wondered? But they were ordering everybody out. The party, they said, was over. And it wasn't up for debate.

But Gina, being Gina, needed to know if that kid was okay. "Who got shot?" she asked one of the bouncers. "Is he alright?"

"It was just a pellet gun," said the bouncer. "Couple of kids playing around. And he's fine. Now go. The party's over," he said again.

"Pellet gun my ass," Kim whispered to Gina. "I know a gunshot when I hear one."

But Gina didn't care. If that was how they were characterizing it, then that was their business. She was getting out of there. She didn't have to be told twice.

Still feeling the fullness of that wonderful man she knew as Ross deep inside of her, and not thinking about the consequences because her whole focus was on getting out of there, she grabbed Kim's arm and they, like a lot of the kids at the party, fled. They left in a hurry. They left and didn't look back.

It would mark the last time Kim ever begged Gina to go to a frat party with her ever again.

It would also mark fifteen years before Gina would see that man she knew as Ross, the man with the arrow tattoo, for the second time in her life.

CHAPTER ONE

Fifteen Years Later

Carmine Serrano grabbed the terrified bookie, put a gun to his head, and leaned him halfway out of the fourth-floor window. "Does it look like I'm fucking with you?" he yelled. "Does it look like I'm trying to fuck with you?"

"I'm not trying to do nothin' to you, Carmine!"

"Now answer my question. You answered your own damn question, answer mine. Does it look like I'm trying to fuck with your ass?"

"No!" the bookie yelled back at him. "No."

"Then stop fucking with me!" Carmine yelled at the older man. "I'm tired of you rat-bastards fucking with me!" Then he pressed the gun harder against the man's head, as if he might pull the trigger.

"I'm sorry what happened, Carmine," the man pleaded with him. "It won't happen again I swear. I'm sorry!"

James Serrano was in the Chicago office with Carmine and the bookie. In his tailored suit, he was leaned against the side wall, his legs crossed at the ankles and his big arms folded as if he knew his big brother was all bark and no bite and would let that bookie go in the end.

And he was right. Carmine removed his gun and then pulled the bookie's upper body back into the office. And it was Carmine who was breathing heavily, more because of his stocky frame than because of any real physical exertion. The bookie was just scared.

"You got two days," Carmine said to the bookie. "Two days to get me every dime you owe me. Not this half shit you handed me. I want all of it! Or your ass will be eating concrete before this week is out. Am I making myself clear enough for your ass?"

"I'll have it. I'll have every dime. You know me, Carmine. I promise you, I'll have every dime."

But then the bookie just stood there, staring at Carmine.

Carmine frowned. "What's your problem? What are you still standing here like a wooden soldier for? Go get my money!"

The bookie reached down, grabbed the hat that had fallen off of his head when Carmine had grabbed him, and all but ran out of that office, nodding at James as if he was scared of him too. They were upstairs, in a massive office building Carmine owned, and the bookie knew, had it been James in charge, he would have been a goner.

"I'll bet he won't pull that shit again," Carmine said, tossing his gun onto the desk and then sitting behind it.

But James had a different take. "He wouldn't have pulled it in the first place if he didn't know he could roll you. You need to stop letting them get away with that shit, Carmine. It's bad for business."

Carmine looked at his brother and chuckled. "And they call your ass *Gentleman* James. Yeah right!"

"What are you talking? I'm only stating a fact."

"You're stating an opinion," said Carmine. "That ain't no fact. That's your opinion. Didn't they teach you the difference at those Ivy League schools I paid for?"

"That's why I'm your attorney. To give you my opinion. Unless I'm mistaken."

"You're my lawyer," said Carmine. "My spokesman. My *consigliere*. And in every one of those cases I pay you to advise me, not to give fucking opinions. I want opinions I can yell out the window. I'll get all the opinions I need."

James didn't bother to respond to that. He knew giving advice versus giving an opinion was a distinction without a difference, but trying to reason with his big brother was like trying to reason with steel. Besides, his brother was no coldblooded killer, despite his profession, and he loved that about him. "And you called me here why?" he asked him.

Carmine leaned back in his swivel chair. "Be careful out there. It's a little murky right now."

"What's happened?" James asked.

"Nothing yet. But there's this talk going around that some assholes think they can take me on."

"With all these second chances you're constantly giving everybody," said James. "I'm not surprised!"

"Your ass just be careful," Carmine said. "Quit with the opinions and be careful! You don't take life seriously enough."

"Alright already," James said to his worrisome brother. "I'll be careful."

Carmine exhaled. "I'm putting a detail on you just in case."

James frowned. "A security detail?"

"Just in case."

"I can handle myself, Carmine."

"I didn't say you couldn't. When did I say you couldn't?"

"But you're putting a detail on me anyway?"

Carmine didn't hesitate. "Yes."

James knew he could take care of himself, and Carmine knew it too. But he didn't argue the point. Carmine was like a mother hen sometimes. "It's that serious?" James asked.

"No," Carmine responded. "Not yet. And I'm not going to let it get to that point. But I'm not taking any chances. Not with you, and not with Vincent either. You and Vinny's all I got."

James's heart squeezed when his brother said that. Not because he was an emotional man like Carmine, but because he saw it as a sad state of affairs when a man Carmine's age only had his two brothers to sustain him. Not a wife. Not kids. Just his brothers.

"I'm taking no chances," Carmine said again. "Not until I'm certain there's no definable threat and it's just a bunch of talk. Which it usually is, by the way."

"Do you know who these talkers are?" James asked.

"I don't know no more than what I'm telling you. That's why I don't like it. It's not from the usual suspects. It's not any of my usual enemies. That's why I'm taking what you call precautions."

James smiled. To look at Carmine was to think of the stereotypical mob boss, even down to the heavy urban-Italian accent. He had that look no matter how he tried to disguise it behind the cloak of his various businesses. But he was a loveable boss. To know him, to James, was to love him. "Okay," James said. "I'll be careful. Just make sure Vinny's being careful too."

But Carmine frowned. "What are you talking? Vinny knows careful better than you ever will. He's in the game. He's right by my side learning from the best. Your ass the one decided to go the straight and narrow."

"Decided?" James asked. "As if you gave me a choice! Since I was a kid you said I was going the straight and narrow or else. You told Pop he wasn't dragging me into the family business no matter what."

Carmine chuckled. "And your stupid ass believed me," he said.

Even James had to smile at that. "Fuck you," he said, and Carmine laughed.

"Anything else?" James asked as he stood erect. "I am a working man on that straight and narrow after all."

"Naw, that's it," said Carmine. "Just take care of yourself. Just be careful."

"You know I will," James said as he buttoned his suit coat. He looked at his brother. "You be careful too."

Carmine was not an affectionate man. None of the Serrano brothers were. But Carmine was an emotional man who appreciated his brother's concern. "I was born careful," he said.

James smiled. "That's lame. Real lame." And then he left the office.

But when he closed the door behind him, his hand remained on the knob. Three brothers, he thought, with not one wife between them. No children between them either. All they had were each other and, James knew, their own personal loneliness. All because of the train wreck that was their parents. All because of the example they showed them that made them certain they never wanted to walk down that road with anybody.

But none of them were getting any younger. Especially Carmine and James. James was in his early forties, and Carmine was pushing fifty. And for James, it wasn't so easily dismissed anymore. He was no longer so certain that those proud Serrano bachelor brothers did it right. He was beginning to wonder if they'd done it all wrong.

You and Vinny's all I got, his middle-aged brother proudly proclaimed. But to James, it wasn't anything to be proud of. To James, it was the saddest thing he'd heard in a long, long time.

GENTLEMAN JAMES AND GINA

CHAPTER TWO

The Toyota Camry stopped at the curb at the private school in Thatches, Illinois and Gina Griffin looked at her young daughter. A typical teen, some might say, with all the attitude and angst of that generation, but that wasn't what Gina was saying. Her daughter was not going to become a statistic, was what was foremost on her mind, no matter how much her daughter hated her for being so hands-on. "See you later, alligator," she said to her.

Tamira Griffin grabbed her bookbag.

"No after while, crocodile?" Gina asked.

"Why can't I spend the night at Tonya's, Ma?" Tamira asked instead.

Gina sighed. "I'm not going through that again with you, Tam."

"But why can't I just do it?"

"I told you to have Tonya's mother phone me. Didn't I tell you that? Have her mama call me. Then I'll see."

"What do you need to talk to her mother for? I'm fifteen years old! My word should be enough."

"I'm not playing with you little girl," Gina made plain. "Either her mother phones me about this sleepover, or there will be no sleepover. You understand me?

Tamira sighed. Her mother didn't play. Unlike her friends' parents, her mother didn't let shit get by her.

And, true to form, Gina did not back down. "You understand me?" she asked her again.

"Yes! I get it. But I don't see where that's necessary."

"Then I don't see where a sleepover is necessary, which ends that discussion."

Tamira rolled her eyes and began getting out of the car. She had her mother's dark-green eyes and curly hair, but she had a lighter hue than her mother. A hue that denoted her biracial pedigree.

"Be good," Gina said, but Tamira closed the door and didn't respond. Gina pressed down the window. "Hey!"

Tamira reluctantly turned around and looked.

"I just don't want you to make the same mistakes I made," Gina said. "That's why I'm hard on you."

Tamira frowned. "But you didn't make any mistakes. You're a lawyer."

"Yeah, a lawyer barely able to pay the rent on my law office. Or the mortgage. Or the tuition for this school. It's been nothing but a struggle for me because it started as a struggle. I don't want that for you. I want better for you. You understand that, don't you, Tam?"

Tamira was a lot of things, but stupid wasn't one of them. She knew her mother, in the end, had her best interest at heart. "Yes, ma'am," she said. "I understand."

Gina's heart relaxed a little more. "You're an honor student," she said to her only child. "Act like one."

Tamira managed to smile at her mother, and then she headed into the double doors of the private school that cost Gina an arm and a leg to keep her in.

And then Gina took off to a meeting with a group of angry clients who, just last night, wanted to fire her.

CHAPTER THREE

Kim McCoy stood outside of the small union hall with an arm full of folders and frayed nerves dealing with those stubborn clients as Gina's Camry kicked up dust driving across the gravel and dirt parking lot.

Every time Gina laid eyes on her paralegal, she thought about their days in college when Kim was this poor little rich girl relying on her father's fortune to the exclusion of any other plans. Gina was the one who got kicked out of their private college and ended up going the community college route, and then transferring to a state university, and then to law school.

Kim, instead, dropped out of their private college with the unhidden intention of living off of her daddy's money for the rest of her life. But when the recession hit and her father, in real estate, went bankrupt and lost everything, she ended up starting over. Only she didn't know how to start over. She never *started* in the first place to know how to start over. When it all nearly went completely off the rails, and she was deserted by all of those uppity-muck friends she thought she had, she called on her old reliable friend Gina. And Gina took her in and, after Gina graduated law school, she eventually trained her as her paralegal, even though she could barely afford to hire one.

But to even Gina's surprise, Kim turned into the best and most dutiful paralegal she could have ever hoped to have.

When the car stopped, Kim hurried up to it. "Be prepared for ugly," she said as Gina opened the door and stepped out.

"It's still bad?" Gina asked. "They haven't calmed down from last night's meeting?"

"Not in the least," said Kim. "They're out for blood, girl. And guess whose? Yours! They want you good and gone."

Gina let out a harsh exhale as she grabbed her briefcase from off of her backseat. "What's all of that?" she asked Kim, looking at her arms.

"Background on similar cases to theirs. I tried to present them to them while we were waiting on you, to give them a more realistic perspective, but they nearly yelled me out of the room."

"Well damn," Gina said. "What they

expect?"

"A miracle, girl. They want you to win them millions of dollars, and they want that money now."

"That's impossible."

"But that's how they're thinking, GG. That's how easy they think this is."

Gina shook her head. They had a good case, but it was by no means a slam dunk. "Well," Gina said as she closed her car door, "what will be will be. Let's just get it over with," she added, and was about to head toward the entrance.

But Kim stopped her. "Not this time, GG."

"What do you mean?"

"You've got to convince them to keep us on, or we'll in serious trouble. I mean serious trouble. We could lose everything."

Gina could tell the very thought of going back down to zero frightened Kim, who was still getting over what happened to her father, although it happened years ago.

"We have other prospects, stop worrying," Gina said to her friend as they walked.

"That's the thing," said Kim. "If these fools in that union hall fire us, we got nothing on the horizon. Not right now."

Gina looked at her. "What do you mean?

What about the Dover case? We still have that in the works."

"Had is the operative word here," said Kim. "We *had* the Dover case."

"They bailed on us?"

"Sure did. Real fast."

"But why?"

"That new law firm in town! It's bigger, it's shinier, it's black like us, but it's making promises they know they can't keep. But they want every case they can get their hands on in Thatches and Chicago, too, while they're at it."

Gina hadn't expected to lose the Dover case. "What about the Lowry case?" she asked. "That case is still ours."

But Kim shook her head. "No, it's not either."

Gina stopped walking and looked at Kim, causing Kim to stop walking too. "What's the story there?"

"Same story. They said they want a team of lawyers representing them and not some, and I quote, 'broke-ass lady with no flash,' unquote."

"Flash?"

"That's what they said. And that's what our clients in this hall are saying too. Roosevelt said one of those new lawyers drives a Bentley. As if that makes him better than us."

Gina shook his head.

"If we lose this case," Kim said, "we'll have zero cases in the pipeline. What are we going to do, GG?"

"I'll have to find work however way I can. I could always get a public defender appointment."

"Don't count on it," said Kim. "I called downtown this morning to try to get you some public defender work, but they have nothing. I called Chicago too. Nothing for us there either."

"Nothing? Are you joking? The public defender's office is always overwhelmed. There's always a case where the judge wants a private firm to handle it."

"But all of those big firms, including that new firm, are going after that work too. In this long-ass recession, everybody's scared. And all of our bills are due. The clients that owe us don't want to pay up. I've been trying to collect, but you can't get blood from a turnip. You've got to convince them to keep us on, G. There's no two ways about it."

Gina knew it too now, as they headed into the hall.

It was a small, rundown facility that wasn't a union hall anymore. The big bosses busted up the unions in Thatches years ago. But it was still as good a meeting place as any in town, and the clients were sitting on a long bench against the wall. All poor. All black or Hispanic. All thinking that their case is open and shut and they plan on getting one of the largest paydays in the history of Thatches.

"I understand you still have some questions," said Gina.

"We got plenty questions," said Roosevelt, their leader.

"I'm listening?"

"Why should we keep you? That fancy new firm promising us a victory and a fat paycheck within the week."

Gina was shaking her head. "They're lying to you. They can't promise you any such thing, and there's no way you will get a paycheck by the end of the week. They know what they're doing. All they want is to get your name on that dotted line, and then they'll tell you the truth. And the truth is this: you have a good case of wrongful termination and discrimination. Harassment too. But it's no slam dunk. We'll need to get our ducks in a row. We'll need to be prepared for trial."

"We don't wanna go to no trial!" said Harriet. "Don't you get what we trying to tell you? We don't want that! We want a fat paycheck and we want it now!"

They all agreed with her, and Kim and Gina exchanged a glance.

"All I'm trying to tell you is the truth," Gina said. "This is not going to be over tomorrow. It just isn't. That's not how the law works. Even if we settle out of court, that's not how the law works."

"It is if you have a team of lawyers," said Roosevelt, "like that other firm does."

And his fellow coworkers agreed with him again. And Gina knew she had to change her strategy. "You're right," she said.

They all looked at her.

"We're right?"

"You're absolutely right. I can't tell you to stay with me. Because I am just one lawyer. But I'm one lawyer who has cleared her books to make certain she only has this one case that I'll work on day and night. They may be a team of lawyers, but they already are overwhelmed with cases. Cases with much bigger paydays than yours will ever be. They'll get around to your case when they get around to it. You know how the big boys operate. But if that's what you all want, then I can't speak against it. Even though," she added, "we do have a contract."

Their talk had slowed considerably, and Kim wanted to smile. Gina did it again, she thought.

"We're gonna have to think about this," Roosevelt said. "I'm a no, but some wanna give you a chance."

"She's been on the case from the beginning. Why would we give that up to start over with another lawyer?" one of them asked.

"But what has she done on the case?" another worker said. "Nothing. A big nothing."

That wasn't true, but Gina didn't argue with him.

"We'll let you know our decision when we reach it," Roosevelt said.

"Okay," said Gina, and she and Kim left.

Once outside, Kim exhaled. "That is so whacked. Hard as you work for them. They shouldn't treat you like this. It's so not fair."

"It's their right," Gina said as they walked to her car.

"But if they drop you . . ." Kim looked at Gina.

Gina looked at Kim. "I know. We're screwed if they drop me. I know." She opened her car door.

"So what will we do?" Kim asked.

"Pray. Believe. God's got in all in control."

Kim smiled. "GG Griffin. The eternal optimist."

Gina smiled, too, and got in her car, but she was hardly feeling optimistic. And then her cell phone rang.

Gina looked at the Caller ID. It was the factory's corporate office. "It's them," she said to Kim and answered quickly. "Yes, hello?"

"Is this Ms. Griffin?"

"Yes, it is."

"Mr. Donovan's attorney would like for you to meet with him."

"May I ask what this is about?"

"The case of course."

Kim smiled and hit Gina happily.

"Yes, I can meet with him," Gina said. "May I ask when he wishes to meet?"

"Today of course. At the corporate office here in Chicago. He expects you by ten a.m." And then the call ended.

Gina looked at her phone and shook her head. "Must be nice to be able to be so arrogant."

"By ten indeed!" said Kim. "Some people are so rude. Imagine us commanding Donovan's attorney to Thatches by ten."

"Right, yeah? Wouldn't happen," said Gina.

"But what do they want?" Kim asked. "A settlement surely?"

"What else could it be?"

"Oh, that's fantastic, GG! Shall I tell the workers?"

"No. Please don't. Not until I can confirm

that's what this meeting is about. We don't want to give them false hope like our competitors are doing."

Kim nodded. "You are so right. I totally forgot."

Gina sat there, thanking God and thinking about her strategy going forward. She had demands, but did she need to tweak them? She didn't want to scare them away from the settlement table!

But Kim grew impatient. "Well go!" she insisted. "What are you waiting for? They expect you by ten. That's an hour drive at least in traffic, and it's already eight-thirty."

Gina realized it, too, and then she took off.

Finally, she felt, they were getting somewhere.

CHAPTER FOUR

James Serrano looked at his Rolex again as he stood at the window of Mike Donovan's Chicago office. "Where the hell is she?" he asked.

"Be patient, Jimmy. She's coming in from Thatches, where the factory's located and those damnable workers. That's not around the corner. It's an hour drive."

"She had an hour-and-a-half to get here."

"In traffic it could take that long."

James exhaled. It wasn't as if he had time on his hands to be bothered like this. He had to be in court by noon on another multi-million-dollar corporate lawsuit. Just a different one of his brother's corporations. Carmine also owned the factory in question, although Donovan handled the day-to-day operations and was his front man.

But then a Toyota Camry pulled into the driveway of the office building and James wondered if that could be her. And then a woman stepped out.

"Describe her," James said to Donovan.

"Describe who?"

"This lawyer we're waiting for."

"Oh," said Donovan. "She's Black or African-American, or whatever they call'em these days."

James waited for more. When he didn't get more, he looked at Donovan. "What's your problem? All you know is ethnicity? Describe her."

"She's medium height," Donovan said, and James turned back around looking at her.

"She's nicely stacked I guess you could say," Donovan continued. "Wears her hair big and curly most of the time, but sometimes straight. I guess you'd call her very good looking." Then he smiled. "If you go for that sort of thing."

James found her most attractive. He went for that sort of thing. And as she grabbed her briefcase from out of her car and began hurrying toward the entrance, stepping high in her high heels and her above-the-knee skirt that bounced as she walked, he smiled. She was all legs, the way he saw her. She could use some meat on those bones, if you ask him, although she was by no means skinny. But she was small. For a big man like him, he'd crush her in bed.

In bed? Really James? Why on earth

would you be thinking about bedding that woman when you hadn't even met her yet! Was he ever going to change his ways? Was he ever going to break out of that pathetic Serrano woman-chasing mode and finally settle down? He never would, he knew, if he kept on the way he was keeping on.

But he couldn't see how he could help himself. Because just like her skirt, her long, curly hair was bouncing, too, in a way that framed her dark-brown face as if it were a picture to behold. And even from where he stood, looking down at her from a window upstairs, she was certainly pretty as a picture.

And then she disappeared under the building's awning.

"She's on her way up now," James said.

"Good," Donovan said, rising and buttoning his suit coat. "Let's get this over with!"

Donovan made his way over to the conference table where a team of lawyers, all of whom worked for James's law firm in Chicago, were already assembled and ready. James remained where he stood, still looking out the window with his arms folded. He didn't usually show up for preliminary talks until the day of trial, if there ever was a trial, but the money amount was what gave him pause. Those workers filed a fifty-million-dollar lawsuit against the factory for wrongful termination, discrimination, and widespread worker abuse. He had to make sure they crushed that lawsuit in its infancy with a minimal settlement payout. That was why he was there.

Gina didn't know who was behind that door when the secretary told her to go on in; that they were waiting for her. But when she opened the door, she was surprised. She had expected Donovan and his attorney, a man named Ruskin. He was the only one she'd been dealing with. But she, instead, saw Donovan, Ruskin, and four other attorneys seated at the table. And they all looked as if they'd been practicing law almost as long as she'd been alive. There was another man, further over with his back to everybody, looking out the window. Was he an attorney too? She immediately felt a little intimidated herself, but she didn't let them see her sweat.

"Mr. Donovan, hello," she said as she stretched out her hand to Mike Donovan. Donovan stood up and shook her hand.

"Hello, Miss Griffin. Please be seated. I'm not sure if you know everybody."

"I know Mr. Ruskin and that is all," Gina said as she seated in the chair across from Donovan and the attorneys. They wanted to make sure, in numbers alone, she felt, just what she was truly up against.

Donovan introduced the other all-white and male team of lawyers, and Gina pulled out her folder while they all pulled out stacks of folders. Each and every one of them seemed to have a separate big stack. Gina wondered if she had forgotten something! It might have appeared as if she was outmatched, but inwardly she knew she wasn't. She knew her case. She knew she had, not a slam dunk, but a darn strong case.

But as if to rub it in, the big man at the window finally walked over to the conference table and sat down too. And he sat at the head of the table, making it clear, she supposed, that he, not Ruskin, was the actual attorney in charge. As if his presence would further remind her of what she was actually up against.

"This is the list of all the improvements Mr. Donovan and his team have already made to the factory," said Ruskin as he handed over a thick folder to Gina. "As you can see there, it is an exhaustive list."

"Which begs the point," said Gina as she flipped through the thick folder, "just how rampant the problems at that factory were and, most likely, still are."

Ruskin smiled, although he didn't expect

that comeback. "What those records show," he said, "is that we have cleaned up any lingering problems. We also have," he said, handing over another thick folder, "testimonies from the current workers about the improved conditions. They all give glowing reviews to Mr. Donovan and the factory as a whole."

Gina didn't bother to even open that folder. "Your point?" she asked.

"It's over," Ruskin said. "There's no need for this lawsuit. The workers are quite satisfied."

James stared at Gina when Ruskin made that declaration. He was using an old trick: making the case about everything the case was not about, and then declaring victory based on matters not even in dispute. Was she experienced enough, or talented enough, to see what he was doing?

"First of all," Gina said, "all of these testimonies are nice, but they don't have anything to do with the case at hand."

James inwardly smiled. She had what it took. She saw right through that little ploy.

"My clients were fired," Gina continued, "not because there weren't enough fans in the facility or not enough drinking fountains. They were fired for asserting their rights. For speaking out against worker abuse in wage disparities based on race. In promotions that never came to the African-American and Hispanic workers. In all manners of harassment and intimidation because they spoke out. I have it documented chapter and verse."

She tossed those thick folders right back at Ruskin. "You can hand me thick files all day long, with all kinds of glowing testimonials from the white workers who, by the way, were the ones getting all of the advantages from this unjust system. But it won't change the fact that my clients were fired for asserting their rights. For speaking up when they saw the injustices. For losing their livelihoods and, in some cases, their pensions because they refused to go along with something so institutionally wrong. You're going to have to pay, gentlemen. That's not in dispute. The only thing we need to be discussing is how much."

When she said that, the room went still. Compared to them she was young, she was only thirty-three, and they knew she had only been a practicing attorney for four years. They assumed she had a lot to learn. And she knew she did. But not when it came to the facts of her own case.

But Donovan's attorneys recovered quickly. Ruskin glanced at the man seated beside him and that man, instead of handing folders to Gina, opened one himself.

67

"Wilbur Roosevelt," the attorney said. "Three DUIs. Five domestic violence charges, including one as recent as three months ago, just before he was fired."

Gina frowned. "Are you implying that he was fired because of an event in his personal life?"

"I'm only stating the facts, ma'am," said the attorney. Then he opened another file. "Harriet Miller. Eight, I repeat eight shoplifting charges. One child abuse charge that resulted in her losing custody of all of her children. A domestic violence charge as well. An assault charge as early as a month before she was terminated."

Gina shook her head. That was going to be their game? Claim each client was fired because of violating the morals clause, not because of the truth of the matter? She couldn't believe it!

"Alice Williamson," the attorney continued after opening another file. "Arrested on a marijuana charge. Arrested on a crack cocaine charge. Arrested again on a crack cocaine charge. Arrested on a theft charge just a week before she was terminated."

He was about to open another file, but Gina stopped him. "Just get to the point," she said.

"If this case goes to trial," Ruskin said, "and it will go to trial if you don't get off of that ridiculous amount, the jury will eat your clients alive. Not one of them has a clean record. Not one of them has anything remotely resembling an upstanding citizen report. Not one of them!"

"And all we have to do," Ruskin added, "is connect those records to their terminations. They all signed a morals clause when they were first hired."

Gina inwardly felt overwhelmed by their body of evidence. Not because she couldn't have fought it, and she planned on fighting it, but because she didn't see it coming. She expected them to show that their work product wasn't up to par. She was ready to defend those lies. But she never thought they would claim their arrest records, which she did check on and knew about, would come up this early. She expected them to impugn the character of her clients at trial. She thought she had time to mount that defense!

Donovan smiled. "That's why they get paid the big bucks, Miss Griffin," he said gleefully.

Gina glanced at the big man at the head of the table. But he was already staring at her, as if he just knew she was over her head. But as she looked at him, she realized he looked familiar to her. But she couldn't place him.

James felt that sense of familiarity, too, while he stared at her. But his thoughts were more on his own reaction to the very well done take down of her case by his attorneys. He was usually as gleeful as Donovan whenever it became obvious that they had the superior strategy. But this time, he wasn't gleeful at all. He even felt sorry for her, which was usually an emotion James almost never felt! People put themselves out as attorneys, then they had better show the goods, was always how he saw it. But with this young lady, this Miss Griffin, he actually felt bad for her. And he couldn't understand why.

Gina didn't have time to dwell on any sense of familiarity, either, as she felt as if she was in front of a firing squad. And she needed to know just how low they intended to go. "What's your bottom line?" she asked them.

"We will settle out of court," Ruskin said, "and give each one of them a severance pay. A year of their wages, paid weekly as they were paid, and based on what they were earning when they were terminated. And not a dime more. We will not admit any culpability, they will sign an NDA, and we will stop paying them altogether if any part of this settlement is leaked to the public. That is our bottom line, Miss

Griffin."

Gina couldn't believe it. "Are you joking?" she asked. "They were barely paid above the minimum wage!"

"So?"

"So they aren't going to accept those terms! That doesn't address their grievances at all."

"Take it or leave it," said Donovan. "They don't deserve that, if you ask me."

"But what about the promotions they never got? What about the wage differentiation between them and the white workers? What about--"

"Take it or leave it," Ruskin said, echoing Donovan.

"Consider it left," Gina said.

For some insane reason, James could no longer stomach the carnage his able attorneys were reaping upon the young lady. He suddenly stood up, which caused everybody to look at him. And then he walked out of the room.

Gina found it odd that he would just leave when they were obviously winning, but she looked back at the attorneys before her. "What I'm saying," she said, "is that a settlement like that doesn't address any of the factors that led them to file this lawsuit to begin with. You aren't considering--"

"And we won't be considering it," said Ruskin, as he stood up too. The rest of the attorneys stood up as well. "Take it or leave it. It's now or never. You take it, all is well and good. You don't take our offer right here and right now, then all settlement talks are over, and we will see you in court. Take it or leave it."

Gina was so overwhelmed, and so angry, that she stood up, grabbed up her papers, and began stuffing them into her briefcase. They weren't serious about negotiating! All they wanted to do was lord it over her and her clients the way people like them always did, as if they had an entitlement. "Well, gentlemen," she said, "that's an offer I will be happy to leave." Then her look turned as serious as a heart attack. "I'll see you in court," she said, grabbed her briefcase, and walked out too.

But as soon as she stepped out into the corridor, she felt awful. It wasn't that she should have been better prepared. She was very prepared. But she wasn't prepared for what they threw at her. She never even considered a settlement like that. She never considered that they would try to link the character questions to the firings. It never even crossed her mind! And that, to Gina, was her dereliction of duty. She failed her clients.

And to not even bring the settlement offer

before them could be viewed as malpractice too. It was their livelihoods, after all, and maybe they would be willing to accept a year's pay. But on that point, she knew she was doing the right thing. They would just have to fight it out in court. At least they stood a chance to get what they deserved, not little of nothing because they were poor and minority and had little of nothing to begin with. She would fight like hell for them.

But she also knew she had bills to pay, and not a single payday coming in. She also knew she was in almost as much financial trouble as her clients were.

But when she walked out of that building, and began walking toward her car, she felt a sense of foreboding of a different kind of trouble.

Because the big man himself, the one who did not say one single word during the entire time, and who left before the proceedings were even over with, was leaned against her car. As if he owned that too.

CHAPTER FIVE

But Gina was not in the mood. Who did these people think they were? Why did they think that workers were going to go along with their nonsense just because they were rich and powerful? They knew their clients had been working at that factory for years, some for decades, and were barely making above the minimum wage. They knew nobody else would hire them because the factory had fired them. They knew what they were doing. What they perhaps didn't factor in was a lawyer like Gina. What they perhaps didn't factor in was the fact that she was going to defend that lawsuit vigorously, and refuse to settle for less, no matter how long it took.

And the fact that the boss would be leaned against her car lying in wait for her, as if he could throw her some bone under the table (like a few thousand dollars extra or something else for herself) only angered her more.

"May I help you?" she asked as she walked up to the attorney.

"I'm James Serrano," James said.

"May I help you?" Gina asked again.

"And you're Genevieve Griffin," he said.

Gina had not been called that name since forever, and it actually sounded strange to her. "May I help you?" she asked again.

"You didn't accept the offer. Did you?"

Gina frowned. "Of course I didn't! Would you have for your clients?"

"Your law practice is collapsing. You can't afford the rent on your office space. Your home is headed for foreclosure because you took out a loan last year to help pay the rent on your office space, only to now not be able to pay either one. You've tried to get public defender work, but the big boys are putting their hands in that jar too and there's never any work left for little guy firms like yours. You applied to be a prosecutor even, which goes against everything you believe in, but even the DA's office turned you down. You've had too many losses on your record already, they said. If I were in your shoes would I have taken the offer? It would have been tempting."

"Oh, I'm sure that was the calculation," Gina said. "I'm sure that's what your crew expected my broke ass to do. Just take whatever you dished out. But I didn't."

"Good on you," James said, his arms remaining folded. "You did the right thing."

Gina stared at James. She didn't expect

him to say that. But then again, maybe he was just trying to appease her too. He wanted that fifty-million-dollar lawsuit off of his plate. Maybe he'd throw in a few more goodies, nothing major, and expect her to bite.

"Perhaps it wasn't a good decision for yourself," James continued. "Because let's be honest here. Your ass is in dire straits. But if we're talking strictly about your clients, you did the right thing."

Gina exhaled. She hated that he knew everything about her, and she didn't even know he was going to be on the case! She'd checked out Ruskin, but it was obvious Ruskin was not the lead attorney as she had thought. "What is it that you want, Mr. Serrano?" she asked him.

James stared at her as if he were trying to figure her out. There was something about her that made him feel as if he should help her. It made him feel as if he should defend her. He'd never felt that way about anybody before, especially not somebody he'd just met, and it befuddled him. He didn't know why he was feeling that way. "Why didn't you counter?" he asked her. Ruskin had already text him that she'd decided to take it to trial.

But Gina didn't see the point of the question, since any settlement, according to those lawyers, were off the table now. "Excuse me?"

"I was waiting for you to counter our offer," he said, "but you never did. You attacked our offer, but you didn't counter it. Why didn't you counter it?"

"I didn't counter it because the offer was outrageous!"

"That's why you always counter," James insisted as if he were schooling her. He'd been a lawyer more than a decade longer than she had. "If the offer is outrageous," he continued, "then you get outrageous, too, and put your outrageous counteroffer out there. Then both sides get real and put reasonable offers on the table. And then we meet in the middle. But you didn't even put an offer on the table, outrageous or otherwise. You were too busy worrying about how insensitive our offer was."

Gina already felt bad enough. Now she had to deal with him telling her something else that she did wrong! Because Ruskin had made it clear: settlement talks were over. "Is that all?" she asked him. "I have to get back to Thatches."

He offended her, which he didn't mean to do. But he was upset that she let her emotions get the best of her at that negotiations table.

"Is there anything else?" Gina asked again.

"No," James said. "Nothing. Go. It's not

as if I don't have a thousand things to do. Goodbye, Miss Griffin," he said, and began walking away.

Gina watched him as he walked away. He was acting as if he was upset with her. And he still seemed so familiar to her! But maybe it was just his good looks. A man who looked like that probably got that *you look familiar* line all the time. She was just enamored with his looks, she figured, which was also surprising. Looks were the last thing she usually saw interesting in a man.

But before she could even open her car door to get out of there and forget James Serrano until they began setting a date for trial, she saw a car speeding across the parking lot as if it were heading straight for James. Her eyes opened even larger than they normally did, and she stood frozen in place. It seemed like a movie!

James saw that car coming, too, and realized immediately that not only was that car heading straight for him, but it wasn't going to be able to stop and would take out Genevieve too. And suddenly he thought of her and began running toward her as fast as he could.

"Out of the way!" he was yelling and flailing his hands at her. "Out of the way!"

Gina saw him running her way, and

heard what he was saying, so she quickly opened her car door to jump into her car and get out of the way as he was yelling for her to do so. And suddenly she was confused. Was that speeding car the enemy? Or was James???

But she had barely opened her door, even though she opened it swiftly, before James had grabbed her and knocked her away from her car just as the speeding car plowed wildly into the car in front of hers, and just missed James as he jumped out of the way with her in his arms. They fell to the ground together.

The speeding car slammed on brakes just as it was about to plow into Gina's Camry, reversed course, and began speeding away.

Gina looked up and saw that the car was speeding away. She at first wondered why he didn't just finish the job, but then she saw another car came speeding from behind James and Gina and stopped and asked if they were okay.

"We're okay. Go!" James yelled, and the car began chasing after the speeding car.

It was then, when James knew the danger was averted and his guys were on the case, did he realize his body was still entangled with Genevieve's. His muscular arms were around her small body, and her skirt was lifted near her waist, causing his penis to be pressed against her panties. He looked into her eyes. Into her sultry dark-green eyes. But only he saw the fear and trepidation there, which he hated seeing. She didn't deserve what she was getting. Somehow he knew it. But being that close and intimate to her proved too revealing. Because his body betrayed him, and he got hard.

He disentangled himself from her. "You weren't harmed?" he asked her as he moved back.

Gina shook her head as he pulled away from her, but she had already felt his erection. "No," she said. "I'm not harmed."

He got off of her, and then took her by the arm and helped her to her feet. But she was still confused. "What was that about?"

"Probably a drunk driver," James said. "But apparently some cops were on scene, and they're chasing the guy now."

"You think those guys were cops?" Gina asked. The split second she saw of the two men in that car that asked if they were okay looked more like crooks than cops.

"I think so, yeah," James said, although he knew it wasn't true.

But it appeared to be enough for her. She began flicking the dirt off of her skirt-suit with the back of her hand. "That scared the shit out of me," she said as she flicked.

James laughed and began helping her knock dirt off her outfit as if it were the most natural thing in the world for him to be doing.

And oddly enough, it felt natural to Gina too. So much so that she looked at him. It should be strange that she had no problem with him doing such an intimate thing as knocking dirt off of her clothing, and she wondered if he found it odd himself. But instead of assessing his reaction to his behavior, she saw something else in him. And suddenly it jolted her. She didn't know why it did, but it did. She knew him. But how?

She could tell that he was too old to have been in law school with her. And she never had a case where he was on the opposite side. She'd only been practicing for four years, after the long slog it took for her to finally get her law degree and pass the bar, so she would have remembered if she had worked a case with him. But she knew him. She just couldn't place him!

"Now," he said, after they both decided she had been dusted off enough, "that's better." Then he looked at her with a winning smile and big, clear eyes. And when he said, "you're good as gold," she was suddenly shaken. Her heart began to pound. Her eyes grew larger. She remembered him saying those words. But it couldn't be him! Because he said his name was Ross, not James. And he wasn't nearly as big and muscular as this man was.

But then again, she thought, that would have been fifteen years ago. People change in that long a period of time. Many times dramatically.

James saw how startled she suddenly appeared to be. "Are you alright?" he asked her.

Gina nodded, although she wasn't alright. "Yes, I'm . . . Yes. I think I'm just still shaken by that drunk driver."

James's heart went out to her. She looked so bewildered! "It's okay," he said. "He'll get his."

"But he would have very possibly gotten me," Gina said, "had you not been here. Thank you so much."

James wanted to place his arm around her again. He liked that feeling. But he knew that would be going too far. "You're welcome," he said. "But you needn't worry. You weren't in danger. I more than likely overreacted." He said it and smiled again.

Gina smiled too. "I prefer a man who overreacts than underreacts," she said.

James laughed.

"Anyway," she said, "I imagine the police would need some kind of statement from us."

"I'll handle that," James said. "Let's get you out of here." He walked, with her, back to her car. The door was still open.

And Gina felt the willies as they approached her car. She could just see that speeding car colliding, head on, right into her car and she would have been sitting in it! "Thanks again," she said to him as she sat inside of her car.

"You're welcome." And then he added: "Have a good day, Genevieve."

"You too, Ross," she said without realizing the name she had called him, as the door closed her in and left him outside.

Gina was shocked by the name she had called him. Because she was certain it couldn't be him. She would have recognized him when she first laid eyes on him had that been him! How could she not? He would have been, after all, the father of her child! Which made Gina all the more certain she was just overreacting too. It had been a long time since a man had been as kind to her as he'd been to her, and he very well might have saved her life after all. That was what she was reacting to. That was what was driving her thoughts.

And she knew not to put too much stock in the fact that he seemed familiar. She could have run into him anywhere in her life.

Anywhere!

That was why she decided to hang her hat on that possibility rather than the other one. The other one, she knew, would have been too crazy to even fathom. And her beloved daughter would have been involved. And that lie she told her daughter.

She hung her hat on overreaction, and drove away.

But James just stood there. Because he was stunned by that name she had called him. *Ross*, she'd called him. *Goodbye, Ross*, she'd said. He hadn't used that name in years!

He hadn't used it in a long time because it wasn't his name. It was the name he would give to the ladies when he didn't want them to try to look him up after any of those one-night-stands he was famous for. Did he have one with her? Was that why she seemed so familiar to him? Was that why he felt so protective of her?

But that didn't make sense to him either. One-night stands didn't ever do anything for him but satisfy an urge. Why would he be protective of some woman he slept with once? A woman he didn't even remember? A woman he had to have slept with years and years ago if he was calling himself Ross back then?

But he couldn't pull himself to put her in that category. He outright dismissed ever sleeping with Genevieve. It seemed to him that he would have remembered her, despite the fact that he'd slept with tons of ladies just like her down through the years. But he would have remembered her, he felt. How could he have forgotten *her*?

But he didn't have much more time to ponder it because the car that had chased the speeding car returned to the parking lot and headed straight for James. He went over to the car as the driver pressed down the window.

"Did you catch that motherfucker?" James asked him.

"We tried, but he got away."

"Damn!" said James. Then he frowned and looked pass the driver, at the detail chief on the driver's seat. "How the fuck did you let those fuckers get that close to me? My brother didn't put a security detail on me for that shit to happen. They could have killed that girl had they decided to shoot!"

"They didn't shoot because we were right on their asses," said the chief. "So come on, Jimmy, we did our job. We chased them away from you and that girl. And we got a license plate number on top of that. We're on it. We'll find whoever was driving that car. We just didn't see that one coming." Then he added: "That girl? Who was she?"

James frowned. "What the fuck is that your business? You're worrying about some bird? You just find out who tried that stupid shit, and bring them to me. Not to my brother. To me. You understand?"

"I understand," said the chief. "I got you."

"Didn't seem like it to me," James said. "And no more following me around. That's over. I'll let my brother know, but I'm letting you know that ends here and now. I can take care of myself. You just find out who that fucker was."

"Yes, sir," said the detail chief as they watched James walk away.

The chief shook his head as he and the driver watched James head for his Mercedes-Maybach further over in the parking lot. "And people think he's some goody two-shoes lawyer who can't harm a flea, when he's as gangster as the rest of those Serranos."

"I say more so," said the driver, "because he can hide behind the law."

The chief nodded. "Yeah, he can easily hide."

"And why would he get so defensive just because you asked who that bird was?" the driver asked and then looked at the chief. "That car could have been coming for her."

"That's why I asked him who she was," said the chief. "But he can't see shit when a piece of ass is in his face."

"Who you think she could be?"

"Another one of his fuck partners," said the chief. "Who else? He likes those black birds. We just better hope Carmine doesn't find out that his kid brother almost took a powder. That'll be our asses if Carmine gets wind of this shit. That's what we need to worry about. Jimmy's right about that," he said, as they watched James get into his Mercedes and speed off just as police sirens could be heard heading their way. His security detail took off too.

CHAPTER SIX

The Camry pulled up at the parent pickup overhang of the Brennan School, but Gina saw no sign of Tamira. She waited, for nearly ten minutes, but there was still no sign of her daughter. She went inside the school, but the Dean said she saw Tam walking home with Tonya Redding.

Gina was mad hot by the time she got back into her car and phoned her child's cell phone. The call went to Voice Mail. She found Tonya's cell phone number, but that phone went straight to Voice Mail too. She tried to find Tonya's mother's phone number, but realized she never had it. Tam was supposed to give it to her numerous times, but never did. And then she felt guilty for not having it!

But she did have Tonya's address.

Gina put the address in her Navigation and drove away from the school. She was becoming more anxious the longer she drove. It had already been a long day. And that drunk driver, or whatever that was, still had her feeling uneven. She hated close calls! One move in either direction, she could have been dead! And the idea that she thought James Serrano was a blast from her past shook her too. She even Googled him after she left him in that parking lot to see if there was anything in his background that mentioned Bayard College or Latham, Illinois, which was the town Bayard was located in, which was the town she would have met him in. But neither name came up. He was a Princeton undergraduate, and a Harvard Law graduate. He was not a blast from her past. Which was a good thing considering what she had told Tamira about the one-night stand that turned out to be her father.

But just when she began to feel as if her driving to Tonya's house was probably not going to yield any results, since wayward teens would not be going to one of the girls' houses to have their fun, she noticed a small group sitting on an otherwise empty soccer field. When she realized the girls wore the red-and-blue skirts and white shirts that Brennan school students had to wear, she made a fast U-turn, and then hurried down the side street. When she saw that Tamira was in that crowd, she got out of her car and began walking across that field.

When Tamira saw her mother heading

her way, her heart fell through her shoe. And she quickly stood up. The other students, seeing a parent hurrying their way, stood up too.

"Who's that?" one of the boys asked.

Tonya and the other girls looked at Tamira. They knew who that was! Miss Griffin was always interrupting their fun. And they were only just beginning. They were trying to decide where they could meet up later that night to have some real bed action fun. Tamira nor Tonya had ever gone as far as those other girls and boys were talking about going, but they were getting caught up in it too.

"That's Tamira's mother," said one of the girls.

"That's a hot mama," said one of the boys.

"Tamira Griffin," Gina yelled halfway toward the crowd, "get your ass over here!"

Tamira's heart did cartwheels when the other kids started laughing, and she hurried toward her mother mortified. "They're laughing at me!" she said to her mother as she angrily approached her.

"Then they aren't your friends," said Gina. "Let's go!" And she began heading for her car.

"But what about Tonya?" Tamira asked. "I can't leave her there with them."

"That's her problem," Gina said as she walked. "She'll have to make her own decisions."

"But Ma!" Tamira said as she stopped walking.

Gina turned and looked at her. And stopped walking too. "What?"

Tamira was sincere. "I can't leave her there with them. Not with them."

Gina saw the pain in her daughter's eyes. And she understood exactly what she was saying. Those boys meant business. They weren't the run of the mill, let's kiss and go home kind of boys Tamira was used to. Gina exhaled. "Get in the car," she said, and then she began heading toward the crowd.

Tamira knew her mother was going to embarrass Tonya, too, but Tonya would thank her in the long run, she felt. She went to the car.

When Gina made it up to the all-white crowd, she could tell the boys were trying to assess her with their lust-filled eyes. Did they ever think about anything else in their entire existence, she wondered?

And they looked older, and far more experienced, than she at first thought. Maybe a couple were as old as eighteen! She realized more starkly why her daughter was worried for her friend.

"Tonya, you and those girls come here," she said to the females in the group.

Instead of appearing upset, Gina could see that Tonya was actually relieved. "Yes, ma'am," she said, and hurried to Gina's side. The other two girls seemed more reluctant than Tonya to leave the cute boys, but they obeyed Gina and walked over to her too. They all were almost as tall as Gina.

"Go get in the car with my daughter," she said to them, and all three girls made their way to the car, looking back to see what else was about to transpire.

But Gina wasn't taking on any teenage boys. But she was going to give them a warning. "Those girls are barely fifteen."

The boys didn't seem surprised in the least.

"If I find out that any of you have done anything to any of them, I will come after you hard. And don't get it twisted. I'm not just talking. I'm an attorney. I'll prosecute your asses to the fullest extent of the law. And I make no idle threats. You know what you're doing. You know it's wrong. I'll come after you," she said again, stared at them a moment longer, and then walked away.

But if she thought those boys were going to shake in their boots, she was mistaken.

"I wouldn't mind a piece of that sweet ass," she heard one of the boys say in reference to her, and then all of the boys laughed. Gina shook her head and kept walking. And those foolish girls might have given up their virginity (if they still had it) to idiots like that!

But that was why Gina was so hard on Tamira. She gave up her body to a stranger too. Just gave it up because he was so good looking and knew all the right words to say and knew exactly what buttons to push to get her in bed with him. And it almost ruined her life. Kicked out of college. Lost her scholarship. Pregnant. Took years and years to get back on track. She wasn't having that for her daughter, she didn't care how embarrassed she made her.

When she made it back across that field and got into the car, she could have heard a pin drop. Somehow Tamira and her friends seemed to understand just what they almost fell into as well. It was all sinking in.

Gina was grateful for that, but she knew her daughter. The next good-looking boy that came along was going to be the next fight she had to have with her. Those girls were smelling themselves now. Gina knew she still had an uphill battle. But she knew she had no choice but to take it one victory at a time.

CHAPTER SEVEN

He was fucking her. Long and hard, he was pounding that black ass. And just as he was about to cum, he looked into her beautiful dark-green eyes. But he saw that she was crying. He was about to cum, and she was crying. And then he woke up.

He woke up, yet another morning, with her on his mind. What the fuck was up with that? It had been a week since that incident in that parking lot, and every single night and morning after that day, he was dreaming of and waking up with Genevieve Griffin on his mind. And it was always him making love to her and then she'd be in tears. And then her face would flash before him, and she wasn't crying anymore, and that gorgeous smile would light up his dark mood. And that would be it. Every night and every morning since he laid eyes on her.

Now it had been a whole week, and of all the people he could wake up thinking about, he woke up, once again, thinking about her. And he had a hard on to boot! So hard that he had to relieve himself.

Once he did, he got his naked body out of bed and headed for the shower. He took a cold shower just to get the cobwebs out and, if he were to be honest, to get her off of his mind. And it worked at first. He leaned his head back and let that cold, cold water careen all over him. It felt primitive, but relaxing too. And at least his mind was unencumbered with some woman he barely knew.

But as soon as he finished, dried off and dressed in his tailored suit, her beautiful, big-eyed face and small, sweet lips appeared again. And she was laughing again with that million-dollar smile. It was hopeless, he thought!

But it wasn't until he got into his kitchen and was standing at the center island drinking a cup of coffee and reviewing his text messages, did it all change. She crossed his mind again. He was beginning to resign himself of that fate.

But this time, she wasn't smiling. This time she didn't have that million-dollar smile that brightened his mood. And she wasn't crying either. This time, he realized, she looked frustrated. No, he decided with a frown, she looked anguished. As if she was in the midst of some upheaval that could take her down. But he had no idea what it could be.

He quickly grabbed his phone to give her a call. Then he realized he didn't even have her office number, let alone her personal cell phone number. Then he thought to look her up. But thought the better of that too. Because this was no ordinary thing. He didn't have recurring dreams and flashes of females anytime ever. Why was he having such a powerful reaction to her?

He put his phone away, finished his coffee, and sat the cup in the sink. He was going to get to the bottom of this sudden obsession, he didn't care how many clients were going to have to be rescheduled. He had to see Miss Griffin again. He had to see just what it was that was drawing him to her.

James Serrano left his house in his Chicago suburb and headed straight for Thatches.

CHAPTER EIGHT

As soon as Gina walked into her storefront law office, she saw Harriett and Mae, two of her factory case clients, in her waiting room. Kim was seated behind her desk. The two ladies stood up.

Gina hadn't expected them, and by the way Kim shook her head, she hadn't expected them either. *What now*, Gina wondered. "Come on back, ladies," she said, and the two clients headed to Gina's small office in the back of the small space.

"Would you care for something to drink?" Gina asked the ladies.

"No thank you," both ladies said one behind the other, and they both sat down.

Gina sat behind her desk. "How can I help you, ladies?"

"They want to fire you and hire those new people," said Harriett. "Since me and Mae are the two that first brought this lawsuit, and the others came on later, including Roosevelt, we didn't want to do anything behind your back."

"But they said they would give me some time," Gina said.

"You know how Roosevelt is, Miss Gina.

He's whipping everybody up into a frenzy believing all those lies those big shot lawyers at that big firm are telling him. We think they're giving him money under the table to convince us to go along with it."

Gina leaned back and started rocking in her swivel chair. She'd heard of lawyers like that.

"What we wanna know," Harriett said, "is what can you give us, me and Mae, under the table so to speak, to convince them otherwise?"

Gina stopped rocking. She couldn't believe it. "Say again?" she asked them.

"We have babies to feed too," said Mae. "Same as you. We need some help."

"I'm getting you help," said Gina as she leaned forward. "We'll set a date for trial real soon."

"Really?"

"Yes! But I need you guys to hold on."

"But what we're saying," said Harriett, "is what can you do for me and Mae until you get that trial date?"

Gina had thought higher of both ladies, but she realized she was the idiot for thinking so. Nobody had ever yet met her expectations of them. Nobody. Not even herself. "I'm afraid I have nothing to offer but my legal expertise. That's it."

The ladies were disappointed. Gina could see it on their worried faces.

"I just need you guys to hold on," Gina pleaded. "Those big lawyers are in it for themselves. They'll cut a bad deal just as long as the defendants give them a cut to go along with the bad deal. I won't sell y'all out like that. I'll never do that. You have to be able to trust your lawyer and those Slick Willie lawyers Roosevelt is talking about getting in league with can't be trusted. I'm telling you they can't."

Harriett exhaled. And then both ladies stood up, prompting Gina to stand too. "We can't make any promises," said Harriet. "When will you know about the trial date?"

"Soon," Gina said. "Within a day or two."

"But no settlement offer?" asked Mae.

Gina hated to admit it. "That's on the table now? No," she said.

"We'll see what we can do," said Mae. "Can do more if we had money to throw around. But we'll see."

Gina nodded. "Okay. And thanks for coming by," she added, and the two ladies left.

And then her phone rang. She answered quickly. "Griffin Law. May I help you?"

"Today makes you two months behind," Parker said. He was her landlord.

"I told you I'll have it."

"I told you you needed to have it today."

"Just give me a couple months, Parker. That's all I need. A couple more months."

She could hear him sigh. "One more month," said Parker. "That's all I can give."

"I'll take that," Gina said, although she knew that wasn't nearly enough time.

"But I'm not playing with you, Gina. I don't see that rent caught up in a month, and not a day over a month, I'm shuttin' you down. Do I make myself clear?"

He was talking to her the way she talked to her daughter. "Crystal," she said. And then she ended the call.

And leaned back in her chair. She was so frustrated she didn't even know Kim was standing in the doorway until she looked at her.

"I should change my practice from Griffin Law to Murphy's Law," Gina said.

"Murphy's Law?" Kim asked. "I never heard of that firm. What's Murphy's Law?"

"If anything can go wrong, it will go wrong," said Gina. "That's Murphy's law." Then Gina leaned her head back and let out a deep exhale.

"What about Parker?" Kim asked. "Did Parker agree to two more months?"

Gina shook her head. "One month, but I don't know what good it's going to do."

"What do you mean?"

"It's not like I'm going to have what will amount to three months of rent in four weeks. I was hoping to have a settlement agreement to dangle in his face."

Kim stared at her. "You heard from that lawyer?" she asked her.

"Which lawyer?" Gina asked.

"The one you called Ross."

Gina looked at Kim. She knew all of her secrets, including what happened a week ago in that parking lot and the fact that James Serrano had reminded her of Ross from fifteen years ago. And how he said good as gold the way Ross had said it. "No," she said. "Why would I?"

"Good as gold, Gina. You told me he said good as gold."

Gina frowned. "So what? People say that all the time!"

"He looked familiar to you. You slipped and called him Ross."

"I know. I know!" Then she frowned again. "But it can't be." Then she looked at Kim. "And you know why it can't be."

"Yes, I do know. I'm the one who advised you to do it that way."

But Gina was shaking her head. "Nope. Not your fault. I made that decision, and I'm going to live with that decision."

Kim stared at her. "But what if it's true, and he is . . . Ross?"

Gina closed her eyes. "It's not true."

"But if it is?"

"Then I'll have a child that hates me after she finds out, and a man that probably will run away from my child so fast that it'll break her heart." She looked at Kim. "I'm not going to let that happen to Tam."

Kim nodded. "I wouldn't either," she said.

And then they both heard the office door clang. Kim crossed her fingers. "Let's pray it's one of your deadbeat clients coming with a big, fat check."

"Check my ass," Gina said. "Cash only."

Kim laughed, closed the door, and went up front to handle it.

Gina opened a file on her desk. It was a child custody case that was set to go to trial in two weeks. But the father was on a payment plan and was already missing payments. Any self-respecting lawyer would call his ass and tell him to pay up or he would be dropped. Kim called. And Gina did too. But he'd lost his job and just didn't have it. He didn't have it or he would pay it! As soon as he got employment again, he promised to pay. Like so many of her clients always made promises. Then she'd win (or lose) their cases, and they never seemed to be able to come up with another dime. She had about thirty clients in that boat. Kim said she should take their asses to court. Gina tried that too. Got a judgment on a few. But no money. It was a useless cycle when you were a general practitioner who took on every kind of case. She thought about narrowing her focus to only civil suits with contingencies. But she would be competing against every big law firm in Thatches and Chicago, too, for those cases. Especially the winnable ones.

Gina's intercom buzzed, breaking her out of her misery. "Yes, Kim?"

"A Mr. Serrano is here to see you."

Gina's heart pounded. She almost said really? But she caught herself. "Send him back please," she said, and proceeded to clean up her messy desk.

CHAPTER NINE

Kim hung up the desk phone. "You may go back, sir. The office at the end of the hall."

James felt like turning around as soon as he walked into that office, but the girl came from the back room and he felt stuck. Now he really felt stuck as he made his way to the back.

But Kim was smiling and pumping a fist in the air. It was the man from the parking lot. Gina had told her his name. And man was he gorgeous! He was also older than what she had expected, too, but Gina needed somebody older. She needed somebody to finally look out for her. And he fit the bill beautifully, Kim thought.

And then she caught herself. Not if he

was really Ross, he didn't! Because then the shit would hit the fan. Because then poor Tamira would hate Gina just like Gina said. And probably hate Kim, too, who originally suggested it. It was a good situation, but a no win situation too.

And then the office door clanged again, and another nice-looking man walked in. Not nearly as masculine as James Serrano, but no slouch either. But all Kim saw was, potentially, a paying client.

"Are you here to see Attorney Griffin?" she asked him.

"I don't have an appointment though," the man said.

"No worries! Since you're so nice, I'll let you go in without one. Just after she finishes up with another client, I can squeeze you in."

"Is that the client's car out front? That Maybach?"

Kim smiled. "Yes, it is, matter of fact."

The man looked worried. "Then I can't afford her," he said.

But Kim quickly interrupted that. "Oh, you can. He's not really a client-client. I think he just likes her." Then she whispered. "They have a history," she added, and the man smiled. And seemed to get back at ease.

Inside her office, Gina remained seated as James walked in and made his way to the chair in front of her desk.

"May I?" James asked when he made it to the chair.

"Yes, please," said Gina, and he sat down.

He folded his leg across his thigh, but he didn't say anything. It was more of that staring at her routine.

But James was staring because he realized it was no fluke. As soon as he walked into her office and saw her again, his heart actually fluttered. What the fuck was that about, he wondered? He wasn't a fluttering kind of man! But he felt it. He felt something as soon as he laid eyes on her again. That was why he couldn't seem to stop staring.

But Gina wanted answers. Because she felt something, too, as soon as she, first, heard that he was in her office. And especially when he walked in and she saw him again. It had been a week since their last meeting. And although she thought about him often, and kept dismissing him as if there was no way he could be the man from her past, she couldn't dismiss how attractive he was. She couldn't dismiss the fact that he had gotten a hard on in that parking lot. She couldn't dismiss the fact how his arms felt around her.

But he was there for a reason. That was also a fact. So she spoke up. "How may I help you?" she asked.

"So, this is where you practice law," James said, still staring at her rather than looking around the office he was speaking about.

"This is it," said Gina. She had no shame about it either. It wasn't fancy, or even nice, but it was hers. At least for another month! "How may I help you?" she asked him again.

"I understand you still plan to take the case to trial," James said.

Gina was confused. "I turned down that offer, if that's what you mean. Because that's the only reason we're going to trial."

"No, it's not," said James.

Gina was now baffled. "Yes, it is. You made an outrageous offer, and I had no alternative but to turn it down."

"Or counter that offer," said James. "Where's your counter?"

It was Gina's time to stare at him. "What do you mean? Your team said if I didn't accept, it was off the table. *Your* team said that."

"Do you enjoy practicing law, Miss Griffin?"

"Yes, I do. Why would you ask that?"

James didn't know why. He didn't even know why he was dreaming about her. He didn't even know why he was reopening a closed door just for her sake. It certainly wasn't for his client's sake. If he took that case to court, she'd lose. He knew that. He could out-lawyer her in his sleep.

But he couldn't do that to her. For some damnable reason that was beginning to irritate him, he couldn't do that to her.

He stood up. "You have until Friday," he said.

Gina looked up at him, still confused. "I have until Friday for what?"

James couldn't believe he was doing this. "To counter our offer," he said.

"But I already told them I'll see them in court," Gina said. "Donovan won't allow me to get a second bite at that apple."

"Donovan will allow whatever I tell him to allow," said James. Then he gave Gina another look. He felt that warm feeling all over again. He was doing what he felt was best. For her!

"You have until next week," he said. "My office will set up a meeting for Friday of next week. Bring a counter to put on the table. A reasonable counter, Genevieve," he added.

Gina smiled. She could hardly believe the turn of events. "I will," she said, standing on her feet. "Absolutely. And thank you, Mr. Serrano, for giving me a second bite."

"Just don't fuck it up," he said, gave her another hard look for some reason, and then left the office.

Gina didn't know what to say to that. She was grateful to be able to put an offer together, something far less than what her clients were asking for, of course, but something far more reasonable than what Serrano's team had offered. It gave her hope.

And as soon as James left the building, and since the second client had gone to the bakery next door to grab a snack, Kim hurried to Gina's office to get an update.

"What did he want?" she asked anxiously.

"You won't believe this," Gina said, "but he's giving me a chance to counter their offer."

Kim frowned. "But I thought you said it was off the table."

"It was! That's why it's so crazy. But he singlehandedly put it back on the table."

"Can he do that?" Kim said. "Donovan's a hard sonofabitch. I can't see anybody going over that man's head."

"But he talks as if he can," said Gina. "And he's lead attorney on the case."

Kim smiled. "That's great, GG. But I am

mad at you."

Gina was concerned. "Mad at me about what?"

"You didn't tell me he looked like that!"

"Oh, child, I thought you was talking about something!"

"That is something, G. He's got that sex appeal in spades, girl! And he's an older man just like what you need."

Gina frowned. "Why do I need an older man?"

"Oh, you need one girl. Take it from Kim. You need one!"

Gina laughed. "Forget you! I'm just happy to have a chance to get this settlement done."

"But it may not help our situation," Kim said. "It can take months before a settlement pays out."

"I absolutely know that. It'll be a while before anybody sees a dime. Unless," Gina said, as if she suddenly saw a loophole.

Kim saw that look in her eyes too. "Unless what?"

"Unless I agree to settle only if they pay up within five business days, or something like that. I can include when my clients will receive checks in hand as part of the settlement."

Kim's eyes were hopeful too. "You can

do that?"

"I never have before," said Gina, "but those big boys claim they can. Why shouldn't I try too? I have nothing to lose."

"Now that's the truth," said Kim.

"Now get out! He's given me until next Friday. One full week. I have work to do."

Kim smiled. She loved it when things worked out. And she hurried out of the office just as Gina ordered.

CHAPTER TEN

A week later and James was pumping his ass off as the woman was cumming hard, but it felt like another day at the office for him. Like most of his bed action days, it didn't jell for him like it used to. It was all wrong. He wasn't in his bed, but was at her apartment in her bed. She didn't demand any foreplay, and he didn't give it to her either. She wasn't even his type, but was some beautiful dame he met at a cocktail party who was more than happy to let him follow her home. They did it last night, and she alone came then. Now they were doing it again this morning, before he left her for good, and it still wasn't working. It still felt all wrong. It felt as if he was cheating on a wife he didn't have, or he was doing something he otherwise had no business doing. And trying to cum, for James, felt impossible.

Except when he was on top of Genevieve cumming inside of her. In his dreams.

That was why, once he had his pickup from the cocktail party in the throes of her orgasm, he stopped trying altogether. He kept doing her for her own satisfaction. He kept doing her for his own reputation. But that was as far as he could get it to go with her.

When it appeared she was no longer pulsating, he held onto his condom to make sure it didn't slip off, and then he pulled out and laid on his back. She looked over at his big, muscular body and then turned on her side toward him. "That was great," she said with a great big smile. "I haven't had dick that good in years!"

James didn't try to smile. He wasn't trying to lead her on any more than his being with her already did.

But she was leading him on. She wanted to make it perfectly clear that she was more than interested. That she wanted more of what she just had.

She leaned into him and attempted to wrap her sleek body around him. She wanted to cuddle. Which was always the cue James needed to get lost.

As soon as he felt her arm about to wrap around him, he got out of her bed and headed for her bathroom.

At first surprised by his sudden move, she looked at him. She wasn't accustomed to men beating a quick pathway to the exit after being with her. She was considered an expert when it came to bed activity. And she genuinely liked James. But she was experienced enough to know that he wasn't feeling her.

And she knew time was running out for her. She was a beautiful woman, but she also knew, in some cases, white did crack and she was going to lose her looks one of these days. She had a limited time to strike it rich and find herself a willing husband or keeper, she didn't really care which one. But James Serrano, even a blind man could see, wasn't interested in being either.

When he returned to the bedroom and began putting on his clothes that their passion had flung around the room, she tried to put on her best smile. With the covers off, with her arms and legs wide open revealing it all, she wanted to entice him again. And he glanced at her, alright. She saw him give her a peep. But that was all he gave. He continued to dress hurriedly.

And she knew she had to get whatever she could salvage out of that hit and run. "What's the rush?" she asked him.

"I'm not a man of leisure. I've got a practice to run."

"But you're the boss."

"With a practice to run," James said again.

Then she smiled. "You don't even try to pretend, do you?"

James looked at her. "Pretend what? That I love you? That I want to spend the rest of my life with you? I don't even remember your name."

She had heard that he wasn't the kind of man who went along to get along, but damn. She wasn't used to such brutal honesty. "I remember yours," she said to him.

James hesitated as he put on his belt. And he stared at her. Was that a veiled threat she just made? "What's that supposed to mean?" he asked her.

"It means what I said," she said. "A man like you, who runs a major law firm like yours, doesn't need any adverse publicity."

James continued to stare at her.

"A man like you," she continued, "wouldn't want some obscure woman with an ax to grind running around claiming rape or assault or any of those terrible things. Not in this cancel culture," she added. "Not these days."

James couldn't believe this chick was threatening him. The nerve some of these people had, he thought, as he walked over to the side of her bed, sat down, and began putting on his shoes.

She laid there, waiting for his response, hoping that he'd get the point and do something about it. A nice payday would work for her.

Something to tie her over until the next one came along. But he hadn't responded at all. He put on one shoe and then was putting on his other shoe as if she were such a nonfactor that he wasn't entertaining a response.

But then, after he put on his second shoe, he did respond. While still sitting on the edge of her bed, he turned to her. And that chilling look in his big, brown eyes stunned her. "Let's get one thing straight. I came here to get one thing and one thing only, and I didn't even get that. So if you think for a second that you're going to scandalize my name in any way, shape, or form to wrestle dollars from me, you'd better rethink that strategy. Because if you claim what happened in this house was anything more than what it actually was, you're going to be the one to find out what that cancel culture is really all about. Because I'll cancel your ass alright. Permanently."

He stared at her, as if to make himself as plain as he possibly could. "Those options you mentioned. The rape and the assault and anything else that pops into your pretty little head? Are they still on the table?" he asked her.

She swallowed hard. She could feel her throat constricting the longer he stared those menacing-looking eyes at her. Eyes she once thought were so adorable! And she nervously shook her head. "No," she said. "They're all off the table."

Then James smiled a smile that could charm birds from trees, which shocked her. Because that menacing look was gone, and his eyes were soft and loving again. How could both of those looks possibly come from the same man, she wondered.

But James wasn't pondering it at all. He stood up and looked back at her. And he decided to give her a piece of advice. "Never run game on a gamer. Never run con on a conman. And if you like your life, never threaten a Serrano unless you're willing and able to defend to the death that threat. Because I will be. Not some of the time. Not most of the time. All of the time. Know your enemy," he added, "before you make him an enemy."

And then he walked out of her room, and out of her apartment altogether.

But when he made it downstairs, to his Mercedes, he got in and leaned his head all the way back. He was so tired of those one-night-stands that he could barely stomach the thought of another one. His whole night and early morning were wasted. And then she had the nerve to threaten him with some trumped-up rape charge? Was she kidding him? Was that the kind of woman he was attracting now?

He shook his head. He was getting too old for this shit. And then he phoned one of Carmine's security chiefs, Josh "Bronze" Bronson. "Any news?" he asked him.

"Nothing," said Bronson. "The car was stolen so the license plate number we had went nowhere."

"What about surveillance video?"

"We confiscated all in that area. Cost us a pretty penny too. But we're pouring over everything we can find. That car headed east, like it was heading out of town, but we'll see."

"Make sure you do."

"Maybe if you let us go to Carmine, he may be able to put more men on it for us."

"Keep my brother out of this," James said. "You hear me? He's got enough on his plate."

"Yes, sir," Bronson said, and then James ended the call.

And then he phoned his office. "Merrill, my darling."

"Hello Boss."

"Any fires I need to rush to the office to put out?"

"Nothing at present, sir, no, sir," she said.

"Any messages?"

"Yes, sir. Finnegan Works has accepted the settlement offer."

"Oh, good. Get Ruskin to finalize it."

"But on another matter, the Guggenheim case, his attorneys have made clear he wants to go to trial."

James nodded. "That's a good move too. I'll handle that one."

"Yes, sir. And finally, sir, a Gina Griffin phoned."

But James didn't recognize the name. "Who?"

"Gina Griffin was the name she gave, and she said to tell you she's ready to counter."

"Which case?"

"Let me see." After a few moments, the secretary came back on the phone. "The factory case, sir."

"Oh!" Then James frowned. "Is it Genevieve Griffin?" That was the only name he knew her as.

"When she phoned she said Gina Griffin, sir. But I assume that's who it has to be since I see right here she's the only counsel of record for that case."

"Right. Okay. Schedule a meeting."

"When and where, sir?"

James thought about it. Genevieve Griffin. The familiar one. The one, unlike all of those one-night-stands after one-night stands he'd been suffering through, that he actually found interesting. "Schedule it for the Leopard."

"The Leopard dinner club in Chicago, sir?"

"Yes. Eight tonight," James said, and then ended the call.

Gina was what she went by. Gina Griffin. It had been so long since a woman actually interested him that he couldn't even remember the last time. And that name she called him. Ross, she said, which only intrigued him further. Did he hit and run on her once, and she never forgot it? Normally the thought of such a thing would horrify him. He hated running into ladies he'd hit it and quit it with and they remembered him. There always seemed to be bitterness in their eyes.

But she was different. Genevieve Griffin was different in ways he couldn't begin to explain. And the way he couldn't get her off of his mind. He was looking forward to seeing her again. And suddenly, as if he could see some light at the end of that dark tunnel he was trafficking in, he managed to smile.

But then his phone rang, and it was Bronson. They just got a read on the man he'd been searching for: the man in the speeding car.

"Don't approach him," James told his security chief, "I'm on my way. And call my brother. Tell him to meet me there in case I need back up."

"You're asking me to call Carmine?" Bronson asked.

James couldn't believe it. "No, you fool! Are you drunk? Carmine on a case? Since when? Since never! It's Vince, Josh. Call my brother Vinny."

"Oh, right. What was I thinking? Yes, sir!"

James ended the call and then sped away from the apartment complex. He no longer had a security detail following him around, but after listening to Josh Bronson actually ask James if it was Carmine he wanted as his backup, it was for good reason!

But then he thought about Gina Griffin again, and calmed back down.

CHAPTER ELEVEN

It wasn't how James normally looked in public as he drove up to the dry-cleaning establishment on Dial Road. He wasn't at all clean-shaven, but had a five-o-clock shadow that made him look older than he already was. His clothes that were normally always well put together were wrinkled and disheveled from laying around on that woman's floor all night. His thick dark hair was all over his head. And his eyes didn't look well-rested the way they normally looked after a good night's sleep, but red, after a bad night's drunk. But before he could go home and get his act together, he needed to get to the bottom of why he was targeted. Or, even worse he thought, why was Gina Griffin targeted.

Vincent was already there waiting, but unlike James he was the picture of good grooming. And as he stood there leaned against his car watching his brother get out of the car, he shook his head. "Hey there. You look like shit," he said.

"Look better than I feel," James responded.

"Carmine's pissed with you, you know."

James stopped walking and looked at his brother. Did Bronson call Carmine anyway? "For what?" he asked.

"For pulling that security detail off of your tail, what do you think?"

James relaxed again. "Let'em follow your ass around."

"I'm not the one he was hearing chatter about," said Vincent.

"Chatter? About me? What kind of chatter?"

"Nothing specific. Very murky, he said. Some people were talking like somebody had a beef with you, but nobody knew what the beef was about or if anybody planned on acting on it. That's all. You know how mother-*hennish* Carmine can be."

James knew it better than most. But he wasn't in the mood for Carmine's hovering, nor Vincent's smart mouth. After what he considered was another wasted night, he just wanted to get home and relax in his tub before he even thought about beginning his work day. And for that bitch to try and blackmail him too? He was definitely not in the mood.

Vincent saw it, too, and left him alone. Even though Vincent was thirty-three years old, both of his brothers were like father-figures rather than brothers to him, and both treated him as if he was way out of their league. It had always been that way. Vincent knew no other way. That was why, when Bronson phoned and said Jimmy wanted him with him on a hunt, he didn't ask why. Or who. Or any of those questions. He just got in his Porsche and came. Just as he was following James into the dry-cleaners even though James hadn't bothered to say hello.

The Chinese owner of the establishment looked at both brothers as they walked in. She knew the Serranos and knew they were coming. She was the one who called the tip into Bronson. She motioned her head towards the back.

James and Vincent headed in that direction, with Vincent bringing up the rear. They entered through a curtain in the back of the cleaners, where illegal gambling tables were set up that time of morning and where men and ladies too were at those tables gambling. They were so into what they were doing that they didn't give James and Vincent a second glance.

But one man did. And that was why James noticed him. Because as soon as they walked in, he slowly got up from his table and began to ease his way toward the back.

"You see what I see?" James asked Vincent.

"Just as sure as I have two eyes," Vincent

replied. "I think we've got a runner on our hands."

"Go now and get the car. Meet me around back."

Vincent and James looked as if they were still looking around, as their target made a run for it.

"Go now!" James ordered Vincent and Vincent took off running back out of the gambling room the way they came in. James took off running after their target, moving around table after table until he was running out the back door right behind their target.

Out of that back door wasn't the outside of the building, but was a warehouse filled with dry cleaning Chinese workers and reams and reams of the items of clothing they were dry cleaning. The target, and James, had to fight their through those hanging clothes and carts of other clothes and bodies and bodies of tired, illegal workers as both runners made their way toward the exit.

When they made it outside, the target headed straight for the massive fencing that surrounded the property. James knew he had to move faster than he was moving if he was going to be able to catch the younger, thinner man. And he did run faster. And he did make it up to the fence just as his target was climbing it, and he grabbed for the target's ankle. But he missed it and the target was able to scale to the top of the fence, and then climb down on the other side. James would have shot his ass, but he needed answers. And he knew he had back up.

Because as soon as their target jumped off of the fence and thought he was in the clear, Vincent and his Porsche came speeding toward the target so fast that he knocked the man off his feet and onto the hood of his car. And then he slammed on brakes, throwing the man back onto the ground.

"There better not be a dent!" Vincent got out of his Porsche yelling, while James, who didn't try to scale that high fence, ran out of the side gate and made his way around to the car and their target. The target was now on the ground twisting in pain. And Vincent had his gun out and pointed at the man's head.

James went up to the target, grabbed him up as he screamed in agony, and threw him against the fence. "Were you the driver?" James yelled at him.

When he didn't respond, James grabbed him and threw him against the fence again. "Were you the driver?" he yelled again and didn't wait around. He grabbed him again as if he was going to throw him against that fence once more.

"Yes!" the man shouted out. "It was me. I was the driver."

"Who are you?"

"Nobody."

"Your name, idiot!" said Vincent. "He wants your name."

"Billy. Billy Brown."

They both knew that was probably a fake name, but it didn't matter at that moment. "Why were you coming for me?" James asked, still holding him by the catch of his shirt.

"He told me to."

"Somebody tells you to try to kill a Serrano and you just do it?" Vincent asked.

"He paid me to," said the man.

"Who paid you?" asked James.

"Porterhouse," he said.

James frowned. "Porterhouse Joe?"

"Yeah. Who else gonna have that name?"

Vincent frowned. "What the fuck Porterhouse Joe look like putting a hit on my brudder? Why he do something that fucked up?"

"You have to ask him that. I was just doing what I was paid to do."

"What he paid you?" Vincent asked, and James looked at him. What did that have to do with anything at all, was his expression.

But Vincent wanted to know what they thought his brother's head was worth. He didn't back down. "How much?" he asked again.

"Twenty-five grand up front. Fifty when I finished the job."

Vincent smiled. "That's all? *Got*damn, Jimmy! Porterhouse Joe don't think much of your ass."

"When are you supposed to meet up with him?" James asked their target.

"I'm not. He gets in touch with me."

"Has he gotten in touch with you since your little mission in that parking lot failed?"

"Yeah."

"How?"

"Throwaway phone."

"What did he say?"

"The back-in pay was off. He said I failed, so the deal was off."

"Where's that fucking phone?" Vincent asked.

"I told you it was a throwaway. So I threw it away."

James exhaled.

"What we gonna do with smart aleck here?" Vincent asked.

"Call Bronson," said James. "Tell him to get a couple men over here to safe house him.

And tell him to put extra men on the streets. I want Porterhouse found."

"We run it by Carmine first?" Vincent asked.

"No," said James. "Keep him out of it. He's got enough on his plate."

Vincent knew that was true too. And he pulled out his cell phone.

James released their target and made his way back to his car. If they were to believe Billy Brown, Porterhouse Joe, a man whose claim to fame was shaking down longshoremen, wanted James dead. But why, Jimmy wondered. He had no dealings with that crew. And he had no beef with Porter that he knew of. But apparently, he thought, Porter had a beef with him.

But as James was driving away, he again thought about Gina Griffin. And it excited him that he would see her again tonight. It excited him so much so that he called his barber, and scheduled himself a haircut.

CHAPTER TWELVE

Her bed was practically covered with clothes and she was still trying on more. But she still couldn't make up her mind. Even Tamira, as she walked past her mother's bedroom, found her indecisiveness unusual.

"What on earth are you doing?" she stood in the doorway and asked her.

"What does it look like? I'm trying on clothes."

"But why?"

Gina had on a low-cut dress, but she was unsure if it was appropriate. She had another dress in front of her as she stood in front of the mirror, to see if it could work better than the dress she already had on. She was answering her daughter's questions, but she wasn't paying attention to her own answers. "I have a date," she said as she continued to move from side to side to see just how that dress would flow.

Tamira smiled. She was shocked. "A date?" She walked further into her mother's bedroom. "Really?"

When Gina realized what she had said to her daughter, she quickly corrected herself. "Not that kind of date," she said, and tossed that dress on the bed, too, and headed back to her closet.

Tamira plopped down on the bed, unable to stop smiling. Did her mother finally find her somebody that could love her? "But you called it a date," she said.

"It's not a date like you mean," said Gina as she slid clothes on her closet rack looking for the right outfit.

"Then what kind of date is it?"

"A business dinner," said Gina. "I have a counteroffer on the table for a case I'm working on that I'm hoping will be approved tonight."

"For those factory workers?" Tamira asked.

Gina glanced at her. "So you do listen to me sometimes."

"Sometimes," said Tamira.

Gina smiled and went back to checking out her clothes. "Yes," she said. "For that case."

"Who's the opposing counsel?" asked Tamira, still not convinced that it wasn't a date. "A man or a woman?"

Gina looked at her tiny daughter, a young girl who loved the idea of being in love. "What difference does that make?" she asked her.

"Is it a man or a woman, Ma?"

"A man. Alright? Opposing counsel is male."

"Then dress sexy," said Tamira. "The dress you have on is sexy."

Gina couldn't believe the words that came out of her daughter's mouth sometimes. "That's enough, little girl," she said.

"I'm serious, Ma! If you want him to accept your offer, you need to use all of your powers of persuasion to make it work."

"I'm not trying to sleep with the man. I'm only trying to win a case."

Tamira shook her head. "You don't know how to use the gifts you have."

"I am using my gift," Gina said as she pulled out another dress. "My brain!"

"Put it back, Ma," Tamira quickly said.

Gina looked at the dress, and then looked at Tamira. "Why would you say that?"

"Because it's the wrong dress for the occasion."

"Oh, really now?"

"Yes!"

"It's a nice, professional dress, Tam."

"For an old maid spinster lady not interested in ever getting a man, yes, it's a nice professional dress," Tamira said. "But for a smoking-hot, still-young-and-gorgeous woman who need herself a man? No. All wrong."

Gina laughed. "You don't know what you're talking about!" But then she looked at the dress again. "Spinster?" she asked.

"Yes!" said Tamira. "You can do better, Ma. I just don't want you to scare this one away too."

Gina looked at her daughter. "Where are you getting this stuff from? Why would you think I would scare somebody away, whatever that means?"

"Because you always scare these men away," said Tamira.

Gina felt as if she was exposing herself. "What men?"

"The men you bothered to date down through the years," said Tamira. "Remember I've been there for all of it."

Gina frowned. "All of what?"

"The pulling out all of the clothes," said Tamira. "The excitement that you just might have found your future husband. The date. And then the waiting by the phone for him to call with a time for the second date. And the call never comes. And the second date never happens. And the disappointment. And the bitterness. And the clinging to me because you're so afraid I'll make the same mistakes you made and end up alone too."

Gina's heart dropped. "I put you through all of that?" she asked her.

"You put yourself through all of that. I'm

fine, Ma. It's you I'm worried about."

Gina exhaled. "No need to worry about me, Kido. Okay?"

"Just don't scare him away, Ma."

"Why do you keep saying that? How am I going to scare him away?"

"You go on dates looking for husband material. But men don't want to be looked at like that."

"Men interested in being a husband have no problem with being looked at like that."

"They don't like it, Ma," said Tamira.

Gina suddenly became alarmed. "How would you know what men like?"

"Ma, quit! You know I'm still a virgin. But I read a lot, like Steve Harvey's book. Just go on a date with no expectations. Just be yourself and see where it leads. Stop scaring these men away."

"Okay, okay! When I'm on that kind of date, which tonight absolutely is not, then I won't scare anybody away. But that's not the reason why those men never wanted a second date with me. Trust me."

Tamira looked at her mother as she pulled out a nicer looking dress. "Then what's the reason?" she asked her.

"It wasn't the fact that they didn't see themselves as husband material," Gina said.

"They didn't see me as wife material was more like it."

Tamira stared at her mother. "You don't think very highly of yourself, do you?" she asked her.

Gina was surprised by that comment, too, but then they heard the front door open, and then Kim's voice could be heard. "Knock knock," she said.

"We're in Ma's room, Aunt Kimmie!" Tamira yelled out.

Kim made her way to the master bedroom. When she saw the clothes all over the bed, she frowned. "What in tarnation is all of this?"

Tamira smiled and rubbed her hands together. "Ma's got a hot date tonight," she said.

"A hot date?" asked Kim, as excited as Tamira. "I thought you were going to meet that lawyer."

"I am," said Gina, trying on the latest dress she had pulled out of her closet. "Listen to Steve Harvey over there if you want."

"Is he good looking?" Tamira asked.

"Who?" Kim asked.

"The lawyer."

"Oh, yes, baby, "said Kim. "He would be considered very nice looking."

"Then he is a hot date," said Tamira and

she and Kim laughed. Then Kim went and sat on the bed beside Tamira, hugging her.

"What brings you over here?" Tamira asked her.

"Your mother wants me to babysit."

Tamira's big eyes grew larger. "Ma, you didn't!"

"Yes, I did too."

"But I'm fifteen years old!"

"You're fifteen years old who disobeyed me last week. I don't take that shit lightly, Tam, and you know it."

"So I'm to have a babysitter for the rest of my life just because I was hanging out with some friends?"

"Until you can prove to me that when I tell you what to do, you will do it, yes ma'am."

Tamira rolled her eyes. "I sure hope this date works," she said. "Maybe if you get laid you wouldn't be so uptight."

Both Gina and Kim looked at her. Only Kim and Tamira were smiling. But Gina was not. "Get out," she said to her daughter. "That's not funny! Go to your room!"

"Yes, ma'am," Tamira said, getting up. But when she looked back at Kim and saw that she was still smiling, too, they both burst out into laughter.

"Little girl!" Gina said, reaching for

something to throw at Tamira, and Tamira took off running, but still laughing as she ran.

Gina looked at her best friend. "Not funny in the least," she said.

"We're just messing with you, girl. Stop being so serious, dang!"

Gina stood in the middle of the room and rubbed her forehead. "I am being uptight, aren't I?"

"Like you got a rod up your ass. Yes, you are!"

"I just don't want her to go down that same road I went down. I don't want my child struggling like I struggled. Struggled? Like I'm still struggling!"

"I know what you mean," Kim said. "But you did great, GG. You got pregnant in your Freshman year of college. They kicked you out of school. Your family treated you like a big disappointment. But you didn't let that stop you. You went to community college. Then you transferred to a university. Then you went on to law school. All the time working nothing jobs and taking care of your baby all by yourself."

"You helped. You were her nanny. Her unpaid nanny."

"Unpaid my ass," said Kim. "You gave me a roof over my head when I had nothing left. Dad was broke and facing prison for fraud, and you gave me a chance to get back on my feet. You wouldn't take a handout from anybody. You did the damn thang girl. You did that."

"I did it, but I did it mostly wrong. Including the way I raised Tam."

A sad look appeared in Kim's eyes. "But you still made it. While me, on the other hand, had it made in college but dropped out anyway, figuring I can live off of daddy's money. The problem with that? Daddy ran out of money, and I had no backup plan."

Then tears appeared in Kim's bright brown eyes. "And neither did he," she said.

Gina hurried over to her best friend and placed an arm around her. "But you're still standing too, Kim. Don't forget that."

"But I would have been homeless in the streets had it not been for you, GG. I never had looks like you have, or brains. All I had was daddy's money. And as soon as that money was gone, every one of my so-called friends dropped me like a hot potato. Nobody stood by me, but you. You even taught me a trade and gave me a job and let me crash at your house until I was able to afford my own place. And let's face it, you didn't have to do all of that for me. I didn't even treat you great when we were in college together."

"You treated me better than anybody else

treated me at that stuffy school," said Gina.

"That's not saying much," said Kim.

"Yes, it is," said Gina. "Yes, it is." Then she exhaled. "Let's just pray he accepts my counteroffer tonight," she said. "I get a third of that settlement, which will go a long way getting us back on track."

"You looked him up, right?"

Gina nodded. "Yeah."

"Does he have anything in his background we can draw upon?" Kim asked.

"Like what?"

"Like anything."

"No. At least I don't think so. Why would I know that?"

"I thought you said you looked him up, G."

"I did."

"Where?"

"At the Bar Association website."

"That website for lawyers?"

"Yes! Where else was I going to look?"

Kim rolled her eyes. "Girl, Tam's right. You need dick and you need plenty of it!"

Gina shook her head. "I'm not thinking about you nor Tam!"

Kim pulled out her phone. "What's his name? Ruskin, right?"

"No. I mean, Ruskin's on the team, but

the boss is James Serrano, remember? The one who came to the office? That's who I'm meeting with."

Kim typed in his first name. "Spell his last name," she said.

Gina did.

"And here he is," said Kim. "Mr. James Serrano. He is so nice-looking."

"Reminds you of Dean Martin, doesn't he?"

Kim frowned. "Who's that?"

Gina looked at her. "Dean Martin, Kimmie. Dean Martin and Jerry Lewis? The Rat Pack? Dean, Frank, and Sammy? The Dean Martin Celebrity Roasts?"

"I understand French better than what you just said," Kim said, "and I don't know a word of French. You think he's interested in you?" she asked.

"Absolutely not." Gina shot that down immediately. "Why would he be interested in me?"

Kim looked at Gina. "What do you mean why? You're a beautiful woman, and you don't even realize it. And you're smart on top of it. That's why!"

Gina shook her head. "You exaggerate as usual."

"If I had half the looks you have? Girl

please. I would have snatched me a fine-ass husband long ago!"

"It's not that easy, Kim."

"I didn't say it was easy. But with my personality, I would have found a way!" She laughed. "Bet that!"

"Do you see anything about him that could potentially help me out?" Gina asked, changing the subject from any talk of wrangling some great man, something she'd never been able to do.

Kim looked back at her phone. "Let's see. He's a lawyer."

"No shit, Sherlock? You know who Sherlock is, don't you?"

"Forget you," Kim said with a smile. She looked back at her phone. "And he went to Ivy league schools."

"Yeah, I know all of that. The Bar Association told me all of that."

"Uh-oh," said Kim. "I'll bet the Bar Association didn't tell you this."

Gina looked at her. "What?"

"They say here that he's the younger brother of . . ." She stopped reading and looked at Gina.

Gina was mystified. "Of whom?" she asked. "He's the younger brother of whom?"

"It says he's the younger brother of

Carmine Serrano," said Kim.

"Never heard of him."

"Reputed mob boss Carmine Serrano."

Gina was shocked. "A *mob boss*?"

"That's what it says here," said Kim, still reading the information online. "Oh, my," said Kim.

"What?" asked Gina. "Something else?"

"It says he's known in some circles as Gentleman James." Then she looked at Gina.

"What's your point?" asked Gina.

"The nickname."

"So he has a nickname? What's your point, Kim?"

"That nickname!" Kim said. "It rings a bell."

"What kind of bell it's ringing?" Gina asked.

"Mick *the Tick* Sinatra," said Kim. "Frankie *The Monk* Paletti. *Dapper* Tom Gabrini. And now we've got *Gentleman* James. And his brother is a reputed mob boss too? It all fits, GG. Come on now. Because they all have regular professions. Every one of them. And everybody in law and order know they all are as gangster as gangster can be. You just can't prove it. But that doesn't mean they aren't what we know they are."

Gina's heart began to pound. "You think

he might be in the mob too?" she asked.

"What grown man you know with a nickname like that?"

Gina looked at her. "You're asking a girl with a nickname like GG that question?"

"But GG doesn't have mob written all over it," Kim said. "I'm sorry, but Gentleman James sort of does."

Gina couldn't believe it. A mob lawyer? She'd heard about guys like that. But they usually only handled syndicate business. Unless the syndicate owned that factory, which wasn't inconceivable. But could James Serrano be in that category? The man she briefly thought could have possibly been her child's father? Could he be in that category?

And for some weird reason, she actually felt let down. Not because she wanted the man. She didn't! But he seemed so honest and decent. So *gentlemanly*. And he came back to help her when he saw that out-of-control car heading their way. And he gave her excellent advice. And he gave her that second chance to counter.

"All I need is his signature on my counteroffer," she finally said. "After that, I'll have no need to have any contact with him forevermore."

And she kept on the dress she had tried

on despite her misgivings that it might have been a little too sexy for the occasion, and she was done with it. If he was a mobster, she certainly didn't see the point in dressing up for him.

CHAPTER THIRTEEN

The Mercedes-Maybach drove up to the dinner club and James stepped out. As the valet hurried to attend to his car, he entered the standing room only restaurant like a man who knew he wasn't going to have to wait.

And he was right. The Maître d quickly left the patrons waiting in line and hurried to his side.

"Welcome, Mr. Serrano. Right this way, sir." And he escorted James to a window table in the VIP section of the club.

James sat down, ordered his usual drink, and leaned back and waited. He was not the kind of man who enjoyed waiting, but he was oddly excited to see this woman again. He still didn't really know why. There wasn't a word in his vocabulary he could use to explain why. But it was the truth. He was actually excited.

After receiving his drink, he would have to contain that excitement for several more minutes before the object of his odd obsession showed up. He saw her when she drove up because he remembered that tan Camry from their parking lot incident. And when she stepped out of that car with her big, curly hair blowing in the wind, and her beautiful, narrow face, and that low-cut dress that hugged her tightly across her big breasts and wrapped around her smooth curves giving them stark definition, his interest that he feared would wane on seeing her yet again, only intensified. It was no fluke, he realized again with inward delight. He was really enamored with this girl.

And when she entered that dinner club, he could see other men's interest intensifying as well, as if they saw something special in her too. Either that, James thought mischievously, or the way that dress hugged her breasts caught their eye with the same degree of lust it had caught his.

But whatever the reason, she shined when she walked into that club. And it wasn't as if she was trying to shine. That was what also interested him in her. She was no *look at me, it's all about me* kind of bird. She didn't flaunt her beauty, nor use it as some tool of enticement. There was something humble about her. Something genuine. Something that led James to believe, the moment he saw her, that he'd finally discovered what he'd been looking for all his life. The problem he couldn't resolve was why on earth was he feeling that way about her. Why her?

Gina was oddly nervous when she

entered that dinner club. Not because it was ritzy, and it was, or standing-room-only crowded, and it was. But her nerves weren't about where she was, but who she was there to meet.

James Serrano.

Or, as Kim discovered, *Gentleman James* Serrano. The brother of a man reputed to be a mob boss. The man, for a fleeting moment, that reminded Gina of the man she slept with fifteen years ago that produced her beloved daughter. The man even she couldn't deny was as sexy as sexy could get. The man she was now relying on to say yes to her counteroffer and save the day, not only for her clients, but also for herself. That was a lot for one man to bear.

Once she was inside the door of the club and was looking around in search of James, a white woman who had walked in behind her apparently saw that the person she was coming to have dinner with was already seated, and she hurried past the maître d, who stood at his podium, and made her way to that table. The maître d saw her and said nothing. Two other white people who came in behind Gina did the same, and the maître d said nothing to them, either, before Gina finally saw where James was seated.

But as soon as Gina moved to walk past the maître d station to head James's way, the same as the others had done, she was quickly grabbed by the arm by the maître d himself. "Where do you think you're going?" he asked her, pulling her back.

Gina looked at his hand on her arm, and then she looked at him. "The person I'm here to have dinner with has been seated. I was on my way to his table."

"You will wait your turn," the maître d said with unusual bitterness in his voice. "Don't you see all of these people waiting patiently? You will wait your turn!"

"They always want to jump the line," somebody behind Gina said.

"I'm not jumping any line," Gina made clear as she glanced back at whomever made that comment. All she saw were white, accusatory faces staring back at her. Then she looked at the maître d. "My party has already arrived. I wasn't doing anything more than what others just did themselves, and that you had no problem with."

"If you don't like the way we conduct our business here," the maître d said, "then you're more than free to leave. In fact, I think it's a good idea. I'll escort you out the door myself." Those standing behind Gina laughed. One even said *here, here* in agreement.

But as the maître d went to move Gina, Gina would not be moved. She snatched away from him. "I'm not going anywhere," she said. "I have just as much right to be here as anybody else."

The maître d moved closer to Gina, to whisper in her ear. "And I have every right to throw your black ass out of here," he said. "And won't hesitate to do it," he added. "Now you can go nice, or you can go ugly. But you're getting out of here."

Gina looked the man dead in his eyes. "I dare you to try," she said.

At the table, James saw it all unfolding. Since he'd been seated, he'd seen various people walk in, see who they came to have dinner with, and head to those tables without any pushback at all. It was nothing out of the ordinary at the Leopard club whatsoever. It was, he knew, common practice. Then why, he wondered, was Gina being stopped? Why was she being harassed? And why did that fool put his hand on her?

James stood up swiftly when that maître d placed his hand on Gina, tossing the napkin from his lap onto the table, and made his way to the entrance. Although he looked unlike most of the businessmen in their tailored suits inside that club, and he wasn't super-tall at all, but he was a big, muscular man who appeared as an imposing figure as he walked up the aisle toward the maître d station.

When Gina saw him coming, even she was taken aback by how imposing he appeared. And he was moving swiftly, too, like a bull in a china shop. Like he was as bothered by this treatment as Gina was. Only he looked like he could do something about it when all Gina could do, and was doing, was speak up for herself.

"What's the problem?" James asked as soon as he made his way up to the station.

The maître d, surprised by his presence, quickly smiled. "No problem at all, Mr. Serrano," he said. Then he leaned closer to James. "This girl thinks she's entitled to skip the line, that's all. You know how they are."

"No," said James loudly, "I do not know how they are. How are they?"

The maître d was obviously taken aback that James wasn't going along with his maltreatment of a patron. "I didn't mean to imply--"

"Yes, you did," said James. "So let me be blunt. She's with me," he added, and the maître d, and that amen corner behind him, suddenly went still.

"She's with you, sir?" the maître d asked

shakily, surprised.

"She's with me," James said again. "She saw me at my table and was coming to have a seat, just as countless others have done tonight without you blinking an eye. But yet you stopped her."

"Oh, no, sir, that's not accurate. I wasn't stopping her at all."

"Quit lying," said Gina firmly. "You even told me you were going to throw my black ass out of here, so don't even go there with the lies."

The maître d didn't seem to have a comeback for Gina's accusations. He just knew he wasn't about to try and mix it up with a Serrano.

"Don't you ever," James said, staring at the man, "pull that stunt again."

The maître d knew that James Serrano was somebody who could get him fired, or otherwise make serious trouble for him. "I won't, sir," he said.

But that wasn't enough for James. "Apologize to the lady," he said, "so we can go on with our evening."

It was obvious to Gina that the last thing that man wanted to do was apologize to her, but fear apparently drove him to it. "If I offended you in any way, I do apologize," he said to her.

But Gina wasn't going along that easily.

"*If* you offended me?" she asked him.

The maître d gave her an angry look, but then he glanced at James and that look quickly faded. "I know I offended you," he corrected himself, "and for that I do apologize," he said.

That was better, but Gina still dismissed it for the insincerity she knew it was. James knew it too, but he also knew there was nothing more to be done. "Come on, Miss Griffin," he said, offering his arm.

Gina placed her arm on his and allowed him to escort her. When she looked back, those judgmental people behind her couldn't hide the look of surprise, *and disgust*, on their faces. Gina smiled grandly at them, even waved goodbye to them, and kept on walking.

After James assisted her to her seat, and then sat down too, the waiter immediately arrived to take Gina's drink order. When he left, she leaned forward. "Thank you for rescuing me," she said. "It's your second, no, your third time if we include giving me another chance to counter. Do you plan on making a habit of it?"

"Three times sounds like a habit to me," James said and they both smiled.

"I loved that look on that man's face when he realized his sick little scheme to embarrass me didn't work. Again, I thank you for that."

"No need to thank me," James said. "He

was just being an asshole."

"Of the first order," said Gina.

James stared at her. "Does something that vile happens to you often?"

"Often enough. It's as if they think we're going to fold up and cry if they treat us badly, when that's the last thing I do."

"What do you do?" James asked.

"I call them out on their shit when I have to. Or, if it's really ridiculous like flaunting a Confederate flag or some stupid shit like that, I just ignore them." She smiled. "Those Confederate folks really hates it when you ignore them."

James laughed. "But you know what it is, right?" he asked her.

"Of course I know. Racism."

"Jealousy," said James, "born out of a sense of entitlement. And racism. That maître d figures the roles should be reversed and he should be the customer and you should be the worker. It's old-fashioned jealousy."

"It's stupid, whatever it is."

James nodded his head. "Yes," he said. "Yes, it is."

"Well, Mr. Serrano," Gina said as she pulled out a folder. "Here's my counteroffer."

"You don't waste time, do you?" James asked as he looked over her proposal.

As he reviewed it, the waiter arrived with her drink.

"Thank you," she said as she watched James open the folder and look over her settlement offer.

"Are you ready to order, sir?" the waiter asked. When it was obvious James was otherwise preoccupied, the waiter then turned to Gina. "Ma'am," he asked, "are you ready to order?"

"Not yet, no," said Gina, not bothering to look at him. She gave him the same degree of respect he was giving to her. Which was none.

"Very good, madam," the waiter said tight-lipped, and then left their table.

But Gina wasn't thinking about him, nor that rude maître d either. Everything was riding on James's response to her proposal. Everything.

But James took his time, reviewing every aspect. And then he looked at her. "Within five days?" he asked.

It was about the timeline for payment if his client accepts the offer. "Yes," said Gina. "That's a part of acceptance of the offer, yes."

James continued reviewing the document, but Gina could tell he appeared a little disturbed by it. Then he closed the folder.

"Well?" she asked, trying not to sound

anxious.

"You want me to pay up two-hundred-and-fifty-thousand dollars per client," James said.

"Plus five years of health insurance coverage, yes," said Gina. "That will give them a fighting chance to get back on their feet and to get their careers back in order. Because your client may have made changes to that factory after they were served with this lawsuit, but it was poorly run. It was rampant with racism and sexism and all kinds of isms."

"Yes, I had it investigated myself. And it was. But the operative word is *was*."

"But those changes don't change the fact that my poor clients have been gravely harmed."

"They're a bunch of crooks, Gina. Come on. You heard those litany of crimes they've committed in their lives."

"They aren't saints," Gina said, "but don't dismiss them that easily."

James folded his arms and looked at her.

Gina continued. "They've had a rough road. And when you come from nothing, and when you have to scratch and claw for everything in this life, then sometimes you get tired of it being so hard and try to take the easy way out."

"Are you excusing their bad behavior?"

James asked.

"No. Course not. But it's so easy for somebody who had it easy all his life to expect somebody who never had it easy a day in his life to go hard all the time. To do it the hard way all the time when you get to do it easy. Every once in a while, they want to do it easy, too, and they turn to the only means they have at their disposal. Is it right? No. Course not! But it's understandable. That's all I'm saying. I don't judge them."

James could feel his heart really digging on Gina. She seemed to truly have nothing but love for those people that hired her. But was she as ethical as she came across? Because if she was, he was worried, given his family background, that she might not want him. "If I agree to your counter, that'll cost me a pretty penny," he said.

"You?" Gina asked. "Don't you mean it'll cost Donovan a pretty penny?"

James didn't answer that question. "I'll run it by my client," he said, "and let you know."

Gina had hoped that he would make the decision on the spot, but she should have known better than that. She was asking for a lot of money. Nowhere near what they were suing for, but still a lot of money. "Certainly," she said.

But James was staring at her again. And

she saw it. "What?" she asked him, trying not to sound defensive. But it was unnerving the way he was always staring at her.

"Word of advice?" James asked her.

"Absolutely," she said. "I'll never turn down good advice."

"Never put a fast turnaround for payment when making a counteroffer." Then James looked her in the eyes. "It reeks of desperation," he said.

Gina's heart dropped. Because she knew, as soon as he said it, that he was right. It did reek of desperation! Mainly because she and her clients were desperate and truly needed that payout asap, but also because it did show a degree of anxiousness you never wanted the other side to see. And Gina knew she should have realized that before she showed it to him. Why was she always being outmatched by this attorney? She used to think she was a pretty good lawyer, until she met James.

And since James was on the other side, she wondered if she'd just thwarted her own chance of success. "Are you saying your client will see that request and turn down our counter out of hand?" she asked him.

"He could have, yes," James said.

Gina frowned. She was about to ask if she should remove the early payout clause.

"But I won't allow it," James added.

Gina relaxed again. "Thank you," she said heartfelt.

Then James smiled, lifted his glass. She lifted hers too. "To our profession," he said, and they clicked glasses.

Gina watched him as she drank. He had those classic Roman features, from the nose to the hair to the coloring, and he had the swag and sex appeal to go along with his looks. But unfortunately, he also had what she would consider to be the stereotypical look of a mobster. As Kim would say, he had Mafia written all over him. But instead of unfairly judging him to be such a person, she decided to ask him.

"I know this is going to sound crazy," she said, "but could I ask you a personal question?"

James looked at Gina. "You can ask it, yes. Whether I will answer it depends."

"Fair enough," said Gina. At first, she struggled to find the words. Then she just decided to ask it point blank. "Are you involved with the mob?" she asked him.

He had just taken a drink when she asked that question, and nearly choked on the liquor. He sat his glass down. "What?" he asked as if he was shocked. "Why would you ask such a question?"

Gina immediately felt bad for asking it, but she stood by it. "It was on my mind," she said, "and I didn't want to judge you unfairly. I wanted to hear it straight from you."

James was taken by her comment. He couldn't think of anybody alive who had ever given him that consideration. They just judged him to be it, and went on about their business. But she was at least giving him a chance to knock down the rumor that dogged him his entire career. Mainly because of his brother, but also because of his own style and behavior.

But it still was offensive. "May I ask you something?" he asked her.

"You can ask," Gina said, taking his line.

"Are you a member of the Crips or the Bloods?"

At first Gina was surprised he would ask such a question. And then she smiled, realizing why he asked it. "*Touché*," she said.

"Don't make you feel very good inside that somebody would think that of you, does it?" James asked.

"No, it doesn't," Gina said. "But by the same token," she added, "I would expect such a question if I had a sibling, for example, who was a member of the Crips or Bloods."

James understood what she meant. She had undoubtedly done her homework and found out that his brother was Carmine Serrano. And he raised his glass to her. "*Touché*," he also said, and then they both laughed and took another drink.

James watched Gina as she drank. She had a way of fluttering her big eyes when the drink went down into her system, and he couldn't help but wonder if that was how she was going to react when he went down on her. Because he was going down on her. He had no doubt in his mind about that. He had to have her, and not just in his dreams. He wasn't letting her get away.

But to what end, he also wondered. Just for sex? Was that all he was going to reduce their relationship to when he already knew that strategy wasn't working for him at all? He knew he was at an age and stage in his life where he needed more than that. Way more. But was she the one to give it to him?

"Do you enjoy your profession, Miss Griffin?" he asked her. "Or can I call you Genevieve?"

"Or Gina. Or GG."

"Which do you prefer?"

Gina didn't have to think about it. "Gina," she said. "Everything else just doesn't sound like a name I'd have."

"Not even your actual name?"

"Especially not my actual name," said Gina, and he laughed again.

"You can call me James. Or Jimmy, which is what my family calls me. Or JJ."

Gina looked at him. "Really? They call you JJ and me GG?"

James laughed. "Not really, no. But I thought you'd get a kick out of it."

Gina playfully threw her napkin at him, and he laughed again.

James, in fact, felt as if he was having dinner with an equal; with somebody who could mix it up with him and come out on the other side still standing. He only felt that way about his brother Carmine. He'd never felt that way in his whole life about a lady.

Gina, too, felt as if she was able to hold her own with him, even though she felt outmatched legal-wise and maybe outmatched experience-wise. But she also knew he still hadn't answered her question.

"And yes," she said, answering his question, "I love my profession. I thank God I have a law degree."

"You ever thought it would be such a struggle?" he asked her.

Gina remembered how he'd done his due diligence and already knew all he needed to know about her. And she shook her head.

161

"Honestly, no. And it wasn't a struggle at first. I mean, yes, I was having trouble getting my clients to pay me and had to take as much public defender work as I could get just to make ends meet, but it wasn't so . . ."

"Desperate?" James suggested.

Gina had to agree. "Yes. It wasn't so desperate when I first started out. But now they have all of these new mega-firms sprouting up everywhere and taking every job they can get. It's as if they want to knock the little guy out of the water before he has a chance to come up for a breath."

Then she looked at James and smiled. "I guess telling you something like that, a man who probably has a mega-firm, is laughable."

"No, I agree with everything you said. They are assholes."

"Does that include your firm?"

"My firm leads the pack, honey."

Gina laughed.

"That most certainly includes my firm."

Gina continued to stare at him. She'd never met anybody so bare and honest the way he seemed to be. Or was it all just an act? She couldn't say. And not that it mattered. After she left that fancy club, she'd probably never see him again. And that'll be that.

"So what about you?" James asked her.

162

Gina didn't quite get his question. "What about me?"

"Are you married?"

"No. I've never been married."

This interested James. "Do you want to be married?"

Gina thought about it. "Yes, is the short answer," she said.

"And the long answer?"

"Only if I can find my soul mate. I don't want to be married just to be married. I want to be with somebody I can get along with and can grow with and, prayerfully, grow old with."

"Old? You're just a baby!"

Gina laughed. "If you say so!"

"How old are you?"

"Thirty-three," said Gina. "And you?" she asked him.

"Guess," he said, and then nervously awaited her answer.

"I have three answers. Thirty-nine. Forty. Or, if you're in tiptop shape, fifty."

A grand smile came on James's face. "Fifty? Are you kidding me! I look *that* old? My brother's pushing fifty, although he looks around my age."

"Which is?" Gina asked.

"I'm barely past forty. Give or take a few years."

More like give a few years, Gina inwardly thought. And she smiled. "I was close enough. Early forties. No harm, no foul."

"Yeah, right!" James said, and Gina laughed. He seemed genuinely upset that she had thrown in that fifty part, although she was really just toying with him. He didn't like it, but he took it like a champ, with smiles and all. She liked that about him. There was a lot, she was slowly realizing, that she liked about him.

And then the evening progressed with nice conversation and, later, a nice dinner. But after they were served their dinners, and after they had eaten, Gina expected it to all be over. She expected him to say he'd let her know when his client made a decision, and that would be the end of it. But to her shock, he didn't seem to want the evening to end. To her shock, he, instead, asked her for a dance.

It was one of those old school country songs: Bonnie Tyler singing the Scott/Wolfe penned *It's A Heartbreak*.

It wasn't exactly Gina's kind of music at all, but it had a steady beat to it. And, oddly enough, she enjoyed his company immensely. "Why not," she said to James and they stood up and made their way to the already crowded dance floor.

And they danced.

164

"It's a heartbreak.
Nothing but a heartbreak.
Hits you when it's too late.
Hits you when you're down.

It's a fool's game.
Nothing but a fool's game.
Standing in the cold rain.
Feeling like a clown."

At first, they were dancing as two individuals doing their own thing. Gina wasn't the world's greatest dancer, but neither was James the way he was moving, and they seemed to match each other's talent (or lack thereof). But James kept staring at her as they danced, and Gina was returning his stare. And soon he moved up to her, and took her in his arms, and their individual dance routine became a slow-drag, with her in his arms, and she placed her arms around him too.

And this time they danced with purpose.

"It's a heartache.
Nothing but a heartache.
Love him 'till your arms break.
Then he lets you down.

It ain't right with love to share;
When you find he doesn't care,
for you.
It ain't right to need someone,
as much as I depended on,
You.

It's a heartache.
Nothing but a heartache.
Hits you when it's too late.
Hits you when you're down."

As they danced, James couldn't take his eyes off of Gina. He was enjoying being with her so much he could hardly believe it. All those roads to nowhere he'd been going down. All those in bed/out of bed affairs he'd had as if he was still some teenager. Now he had a grownup in his arms, somebody he wanted to talk to and tell his secrets to and protect and love and cherish. He wanted her sexually, too, but for once in his life that wasn't his motivation. That wasn't the overriding reason he wanted to be with her. And it was a shock to his system. His heart did ache! For Gina.

And after they danced, and finally made it to the exit, figuring they'd gotten as much out of their dinner date as they were going to get, he still wasn't ready to let her go.

As they stood there waiting for the valets to bring both cars around, he stood as close to her as he possibly could without touching her. He wanted right then and there to invite her to his bed, but he didn't want to scare her away. He didn't want her to think that was all he was interested in, because it wasn't. But it was a fact: he wanted her desperately, and in every way.

But it wasn't until he had walked her over to her car, and had helped her inside, and was still standing inside her door, did he do it. He couldn't let her just leave. She may not want to come back again.

He crouched down at her door, which had him at eyeball level with her, and he asked her. "I want you to come over to my place," he said. "There's something I want to show you."

Gina could see that he was staring at her to determine her reaction to such a blatant offer. Because she knew that offer like the back of her hand. He wanted to show her something already, and it was more than likely inside his pants.

But what surprised her wasn't the fact that he had asked her. Boys would be boys and they always would ask. But what surprised her was that she wasn't ready to say no. That she was actually entertaining the idea. That she'd been so sex starved and so alone for so long that she didn't want the evening to end either. And because of that, when somebody she felt she had a connection with showed up, it was hard to just walk away.

And that was why she didn't. "Why not?" she said to him.

James was happily surprised that she didn't turn him down flat. He was so happy that he, at first, began talking as if he had to explain himself. "I don't live that far from here, and I was just . . ."

But when he realized she had said yes, he smiled. She smiled too.

"Didn't expect that answer, did you?" she asked.

James laughed. "I was hoping for that answer," he said.

"I'll follow you," Gina said, James said okay, and then he hurried to his car as the valet brought his up too.

Gina was scared as hell, but she followed that beautiful Maybach he drove.

James was delighted as hell, as she followed him.

Neither knew what the night would bring, but they both were hopeful that it would bring more than just a moment in time.

Because they knew, for their own

separate reasons, that they both needed way
more than that.

CHAPTER FOURTEEN

Gina had heard of this part of the city, but she'd never seen it with her own two eyes before. Houses that looked like mansions for as far as the eye could see, all with vast acres of land between them. All up on hills seemed liked. All so well-manicured and magnificent that Gina wondered if she'd died and gone to heaven. But she knew she hadn't. She knew it was just James's world.

Her Camry followed his Mercedes as he made his way along that long, winding tree-lined street to his house near the end of the road. And then her cell phone rang. It was Kim.

"Hey girl."

"Hey."

"How's it going?"

"Tam around?"

"No, girl. You know I wouldn't call you and ask about a date with that child of yours listening to my every word. She's in her room. So how's it going?" Kim asked again.

"I'm on my way to his house as we speak," said Gina.

"Are you serious?" Kim sounded shocked.

"So it's going pretty good I think," Gina said.

"But don't forget about his background, GG. He's got mob written all over him."

But Gina had a different experience with James. "He's okay," she said.

"What's that supposed to mean?"

"It means what I said. He's okay."

"Girrl, that man done rocked your world already?"

Gina laughed. "Bye, Kim!"

"Wait! Are you spending the night with him? Is that what you're telling me?"

"I'm telling you I don't know. But maybe," said Gina. "That's what I'm telling you."

"Well alright. It's your life. I'll stay over with Tam either way, although the girl is more than old enough and smart enough to stay home alone."

"She's old enough and smart enough, alright, but she's also smelling those boys enough that no way is she staying home alone. Not yet anyway. One slip-up like I had and that could ruin her life."

"You're right about that. I hear ya'. I remember how crazy I was at fifteen too. But be careful, G. And let him know people know where you are and who you're there with in case he tries some stupid shit."

"I will," said Gina, although she had zero fear of anything like that to worry about with James. And she and Kim ended the call.

As she was ending the call, James drove up into the long, angular, horseshoe driveway, and Gina followed him. And she smiled. His house was a sprawling Tudor-styled home that reminded her of a massive gingerbread house. Was this how all of those super-successful attorneys lived, she wondered. Was this what she could expect if her floundering career ever took off? Imagine her and Tamira in a house like that! It would truly be a dream come true.

But right now, she was battling nerves. She'd been with successful men before, but none on this scale, and none who made her feel as if she was somebody special to them. Not that she was special to James. She wasn't living in fantasyland. But he made her feel as if she was. Which, she knew, meant that he was either a darn good manipulator, or just darn good.

He got out of his car and walked over to her car as she was opening her car door.

"Thanks," she said as he helped her out like the gentleman his nickname suggested he was, and he closed her car door for her. "This is nice," she added, looking around.

James smiled at the nice reference, as if

she was doing everything she could to not seemed too impressed, but he was used to all kinds. And he knew Gina Griffin was a kind apart.

"Let's get out of this wind," he said as he escorted her up to his front door and then used a keycard to enter his home.

Gina tried not to show her surprise when she walked into his home. Not that it wasn't beautiful, but it wasn't nearly as grand as she had expected it to be. The place was sprawling and big, and the furniture was gorgeous antique furniture, but it looked as if it had never been sat on. The walls were all white. The baseboards were all white. The crown molding was all white. Even the tailored drapes were eggshell white. Gina felt blinded by the whiteness.

James saw her looking around and asked her the question he asked every woman who ever dawned his door. "You like?" he asked her, as she continued to look around, and then he stared at her. Would she be honest, he wondered, or would she be as fake as all the others had been who wanted to be with him so badly that they'd lie to appease him? Because he knew, like they all knew, there was only one answer for it.

"Not really, no," Gina said.

James smiled. She was for real, as he

somehow knew she'd be. "No?" he asked, as if he was offended.

"I don't mean to say your taste isn't your taste, because it clearly is." Gina smiled. "It's just not my taste."

"Not in the least?" James asked.

"Not in the least," Gina said.

James laughed. "Good. I would have truly been offended if you said anything else."

Gina looked at him. "What? You don't like it either?"

"Hate it."

"Then why haven't you changed it, James?"

James paused for longer than he had realized, and then he answered. "My mother picked out this house with me, and I allowed her to handle all of the decorations and any renovations she saw fit. I was in Europe during the renovations, on a messy case that took months to resolve, and she gladly handled everything for me. When I got the call that she had been in a horrific car accident, I rushed back to the States to be by her side. But I arrived too late."

Gina's heart dropped.

James exhaled. "She was already gone," he said. "And when I went to the house, this house, this was what I saw. This was how she had decided to decorate it. And I laughed, thinking what have I done, because this was so my mother's style."

Gina smiled.

"And I cried," James said, "because this was all I had left of her. No, it's not my style at all. But it's my mother's style, and it was the last thing she did on this earth. And she was doing it for me. That's why it stays like this."

Gina nodded her head. She understood fully. "You sound as if you were a very good son to her."

"I wasn't," James quickly pointed out. "None of us were. We were too busy with our lives to be involved with hers. And she was too busy with her life to be involved with ours. Until she asked if she could decorate my new home once I found it. I told her she could. But letting her do this house was just another selfish move on my part. Because then I didn't have to bother with it. I was quite the opposite of a good son."

Although he spoke with brutal honesty, Gina still felt a connection to what he was saying. Her parents never failed her, but when she became a single parent; when she became a *statistic* as her father always called it, she failed them.

James looked over her sleek body. "Would you like a tour of the place?" he asked her.

"Is it more like this?" Gina asked him.

James had to nod his head. "Exactly like this," he said.

"Then I'm good," Gina said.

James laughed heartily. "You can't lie even if you tried, can you?" he asked her.

"It's not in me to go along to get along, that's true."

"Good," James said, nodding his head again. "Don't lose that. It's refreshing."

Gina smiled and looked at him. "Not being a liar is refreshing?"

James's smile left. "Yes. It is."

She realized, once again, he was staring at her in that way that seemed beyond lustful, although lust was there. But for reason it seemed more affectionate than that to Gina. And she found herself staring right back at him.

It was enough for James. He walked up to her. She could smell his cologne. The freshness of his tailored suit. His *man-ness*. "I have a confession to make," he said to her as he placed his hands on her arms.

Gina felt nervous and excited all at once, not just from his nearness, but especially when he placed his hands on her. She realized how big his hands were against her small arms. But his words made her nervous. "A confession?"

she asked, noticing how tanned he was up close, and how his lips almost had a puckered look. "What's your confession?"

"I brought you here on false pretenses," said James as he began rubbing her arms. "I invited you over, not to show you some object in my home. Or even my home."

Gina was getting a little concerned. "Then why did you bring me here?" she asked.

James could feel the softness of her smooth skin just from rubbing her arms. He could see the rich texture of her beautiful face. "I brought you here," he said in a husky, lustful voice, "because I didn't want the evening to end."

Gina was feeling his rubs as if they were a massage. Every stroke was relaxing her even more. And his words calmed her back down. "Why wouldn't you want it to end?" she asked him in her own husky voice.

He continued to stare at her. He had no ready answer. And he wasn't going to invent one. "I don't know," he said. "I like your company. I like you. But I don't know why I needed so badly to have you with me tonight."

Gina was pleased by his response. Because she felt the same way too. She didn't want their evening to end. She didn't know why either. "Thank you for your honesty," she said.

"You're refreshing too."

When she said those kind words, perhaps the kindest thing anybody had ever said to him in a long, long time, James couldn't hold back any longer. Who was he kidding? He was attracted to this lady in ways he'd never been attracted to anybody before she came along. And he had an urgent need to act on that attraction.

He moved closer to her, although they were already quite close, and then he lifted her chin, studied her lips as if he'd never seen anything more luscious, and then he moved in and began kissing her.

Gina felt that sense of urgency, too, when his lips touched hers and they began kissing. It had been so long since she'd been intimate with a man that she couldn't resist, either, and she returned his kiss.

But when she returned his kiss, something inside of James broke and he wrapped her into his arms and began kissing her with that urgency they both felt. And when she wrapped her arms around him, too, it became too much. Their slow kissing became almost frantic as if a crescendo of passion had broken out of both of them and they couldn't contain the fire.

They began moving as if they were one

until they bumped into the sofa and Gina fell down onto the sofa with James on top of her. And he halfway unzipped her dress, removed it off her shoulders, and began kissing her neck and chest. She smelled so wonderful and fresh to him, and so sweet that he knew he was going to leave passion marks all over her. But as he was about to pull down her bra, to kiss her breasts, he looked into her eyes. And he suddenly realized something profound. She wasn't one of his hit and run conquests. He knew that in every fiber of his being. Then why was he treating her as if she were?

"No," he said, as he stopped kissing her.

Gina was confused. Did he say no? Was he no longer interested?

But then he got up, and he lifted her into his arms. You deserve better than this," he said to her and carried her down two corridors that led to a bedroom in the very back of the sprawling home. His bedroom. And he laid her on his bed.

Gina knew she was in the master bedroom, and she was inwardly thrilled that he didn't cheapen their union with some fast bang that would have belittled how they both seemed to be feeling. And the fact that he had moved her to his bedroom didn't slow him down one iota.

He removed his shoes, his suitcoat and shirt, and his t-shirt seemingly in rapid succession, and then he pulled down her dress until it was at her waistline, and he removed her bra. When he saw her big, firm, brown breasts pop out, she would have thought he was a kid in a candy store. He kissed and sucked and squeezed her breasts with a passion she loved. She held onto his head as if he couldn't get enough of her.

It was true. James couldn't get enough of Gina. And the more he kissed her and sucked her and squeezed her, the more he wanted her. She was like the gift that kept on giving, and he began moving down her body with his lips, kissing her in various sensitive places as he moved. When he got to her waistline, he removed her dress completely off of her, and began kissing her little navel. And then he removed her heels and panties.

When he did, and when he moved between her legs, he cupped her ass with his big hands with such masterfulness that she let out a primal sigh that she knew, had servants been in that house, they would have heard her.

He gave her the kind of oral she hadn't experienced in years. The kind that had her lifting up to meet his demand, which only made him go down on her even harder. And she kept sighing and moving and lifting up. She couldn't help herself. He was giving her exactly what she needed.

James loved her taste so much that he couldn't pull himself away from her. But he knew he had to or he was going to cum in his pants! So he finally broke away, stood up, and unbuckled and unzipped those pants.

Gina watched as he dropped his pants and briefs to the floor, and stepped out of them. She watched as his extra-large penis, his already fully aroused penis, began to stand at attention as he looked sensually at her. And she thought how in the world was all of that going to get inside of her. She remembered thinking the same thing before, but she couldn't place with whom or where or when. She just knew she'd thought that before.

But when James's naked body got on top of her naked body, and he began kissing her on the lips again, Gina pushed him off of her.

At first, James was shocked. Was he too hard on her? But when she got on top of him as he laid on his back, and began kissing him as she moved down his body, he could hardly believe his good luck. And it inwardly delighted him. Here was a woman willing to take time away from her own passion, to give some back to him.

James laid his head all the way back as Gina moved down his muscular body. And when her mouth met his member, and she began going down on him with the same vigor he had displayed going down on her, his six-pack abs began to breath in and out in a near-hyperventilative state as he felt the sweetness of her tongue lick and suck and give to him what he needed her to give him. She was so good that he knew he had to stop her before he came in her mouth.

And he stopped her. He lifted her body back up the length of his body, and he laid her on her back on his bed. And then he was on top of her, sucking her breasts again, and then his rock-hard penis was begging to guide itself inside of her. Raw.

He looked at her, and then he moved his mouth to her ear, as if what he was about to tell her would be their little secret. "I've never had unprotected sex in my life," he said in her ear. "Either I've used a condom, or the woman has. I want to go raw with you."

Gina wanted him to go raw with her, too, as she could feel his penis rubbing against the outside of her vagina. She liked this man, but she didn't really know this man. She was just getting to know him. And although she believed what he said, because he seemed genuinely honest, she wasn't about to take that chance with her health. She had a daughter to raise, a daughter who would go buck-wild if somebody else had to raise her. She loved her child too much. She couldn't take that chance.

"Will you let me go raw inside of you, Gina?" he asked her, and nibbled at her ear in such a sensual way that she was ready to toss caution to the wind.

But she couldn't! "I want you raw, too, James," she said to him. "I truly do. But I can't take that chance."

James was disappointed. He so wanted to go in on her without any barriers. But he understood she was being responsible. And he appreciated that even more. He put on protection.

And his penis, still as aroused as ever, guided itself inside of her. And they both felt the heat to such a degree that it felt raw even if it wasn't.

James laid on top of her with his eyes closed as he made long-lasting love to her. When he realized how tight she was, and how much effort it took just to move inside of her, he felt a sense of wonderment. Being with her felt so good in so many ways. He wrapped her in his arms as he kept doing her.

He started out not wanting the evening to

end. But now he didn't want him and her to end either. As a couple. As two people striving as one.

And it felt just as good for Gina because she could barely hold on. With every stroke his penis stroked her with, she was getting hotter and hotter. And then she couldn't hold on another second. Her orgasm came like fire, and she let out a scream that made even James feel her sensations. Which became so sensual that he couldn't hold out a moment longer either. He came too. And together their gyrations increased until the bedsprings were humming a love tune too.

Until their movements slowed, the bedsprings slowly stopped humming, and they collapsed in total satisfaction.

Gina, in fact, was so satisfied that within minutes she was fast asleep.

He was as satisfied as she was.

If not more so.

And within minutes he was fast asleep too.

CHAPTER FIFTEEN

She opened her eyes and smiled. James had his big arm around her and had her backside seemingly wedged against his front. And he slept so peacefully, which made her feel extra special, as if their night together may have contributed to it. She knew it contributed to her peaceful night's sleep. She couldn't remember the last time she'd slept all night long, and filled with such sense of belonging!

But that only meant the bathroom was beckoning her now that it was a new morning, and she hadn't relieved herself all night. She therefore attempted to remove James's big arm from around her, which wasn't easy, so that she could get out of bed without disturbing him.

But she suddenly realized that removing his arm wasn't her only challenge. She realized his penis was still lodged inside of her, deep inside of her, and he apparently had a piss hard because he had a full erection that felt hard as steel.

And to make matters worse, or better, she thought with a smile, was the fact that when she tried to ease his still-condomed covered penis out of her, any mere movement made her sensual again and her body betrayed her. And she wanted him again.

She began to move a little back and forth on that hard rod that was deep inside of her. Nothing serious she thought. She was just getting a little feel in. But almost right away he began to wake up and respond to that feel, and before she could stop her movement and ease her vagina away from him, he was moving too. And like everything James seemed to do, she thought, he wasn't interested in a little feel. He wanted a full blown fuck. And that was exactly what they got.

They were at it again. James was now wide awake, and Gina's eyes were closed as he pulled her back against him and did her hard from the back. He was squeezing her breasts as he did her, and kissing her neck, which only heightened her cum. Because she definitely came again. Only this time she came even harder than she had their last time.

James came harder, too, she thought, by the way he was grunting and increasing his movements at an almost frantic pace. He was pounding her and she was loving every pound. She even leaned back and placed her hand on the back of his neck, to make sure he understood how much she loved every pound, and he responded with even more vigor.

Whatever she was giving him, he was loving it, because he couldn't seem to get enough of her. He was doing her as if he hadn't had sex in years!

She'd never had a morning fuck before, but she'd heard they were fantastic. Now she understood why her friends thought so. Because as James came, she was cumming again too. They came together. And it was such a hard, emotional session that her actual ass was hurting by the time James finished pounding it.

And when it was all over, James turned her around to him, to see for himself that she enjoyed it at that out-of-this-world level that he had enjoyed it. And when he saw it in her beautiful eyes for himself, he smiled. He was back. All of those one-night-stands that had been turning him off more than they had turned him on were over. Because he knew beyond a shadow of a doubt right then and there that Gina Griffin was no one-night-stand. That Gina Griffin was going to be his keeper. She, he decided hastily and irrationally, was going to be his wife.

He kissed her, desperately hard, as if he still had points to prove to her, and then he wrapped her in his arms again.

Gina felt it too. James was the most

passionate man she'd ever been with. And the most caring too. Because he took care to make sure her needs were met even before he met his own. That was a first for Gina. Every other man she'd ever been with couldn't even begin to explore her wants and needs. He was too busy going for self. He was too busy getting his rocks off, and getting them off almost always to the exclusion of her ever getting hers. But James made certain she got hers first. Was he really that good? Because he seemed too good to be true.

And that was when panic set in for Gina. Was she just another conquest for him? Were all these wonderful feelings she was feeling just bare-knuckled lust for him? Was she reading way too much into one night together?

And as she realized she probably was, and that James would hit her and leave her just like all those men in her past had done, she slowly came back down to earth. It was a good fuck. Period. No more. No less. Get over yourself Gina, she told herself. And once James had fallen asleep again, she eased out of his grasp, and out of his bed.

She began grabbing up her clothes that had been discarded through the night to go into the bathroom and pee and get dressed, but something caught her eye. It was his arm. He was still turned away from where she was standing. He was still sleeping that gentle sleep he seemed to have mastered. But that tattoo on his thick, upper arm. And she remembered that design!

But it couldn't be.

If it were the same design, then that would have to mean that her first impression of him was true, and he was . . . And he was . . . It couldn't be!

In shock, she moved closer to him to get a better look. It was early morning and the only light illumination was what was coming through the plantation shutters on his windows. But it proved enough. Because she saw it. She saw that design shaped like an arrow on his upper arm. The exact same design she remembered about the man she slept with fifteen years ago that produced a love child. Her child. Tamira!

And she panicked. She put on her clothes so fast that she nearly tripped, and then she hurried out of that bedroom, and found her way around corridors and then out of that house altogether. She still needed to pee, but she couldn't even think about that now. She just had to get away from him.

Her heart was pounding by the time she got in her car and drove away. What had just moments before felt like a dream come true, was now feeling like her worst nightmare realized. And the tears were streaming down her face.

James Serrano was Tamira's father. There was no doubt in her mind any longer. James was the one she had slept with all those years ago and had gotten so caught up in her own passion that she allowed him to stay inside of her after his condom broke.

But Gina had a problem. Because she had told Tamira that her father was dead! She had told her that her father was dead rather than admitting to her impressionable young child that he had been a one-night stand she only knew as Ross. That she had been just that irresponsible. That she had been everything she was fighting so hard to make sure Tamira would never become. That she searched for him and couldn't find him because nobody had ever heard of anybody named Ross. That she was terrified that if Tamira found him herself, he'd break her child's heart.

What was she going to tell her child now?

What was she going to tell James?

Would they both hate her in the end?

The more she thought about it, the more the tears came. The tears kept coming. She could hardly see the road for the tears.

CHAPTER SIXTEEN

He woke up, after she had left, but he had no idea she was gone. He called her name, hoping against hope that she was in the bathroom or the parlor or even in the kitchen preparing a meal. He even got out of bed, put on a bathrobe, and roamed around his house looking for her. He already noticed that her clothes were gone. But he assumed she wouldn't be walking around naked in his house. Not yet anyway. But when he went up front, and looked out of his floor-to-ceiling windows and saw that her car was no longer parked on his driveway, his heart sank. She was gone? She had abandoned him without even telling him goodbye?

He stood at that window far longer than he knew was healthy. She had hit and run on him, what was so unusual about that? He'd done it to women the whole of his life, why would he think he would be immune from a woman doing it to him?

Because no woman had ever done it to him before.

Because that particular woman, *Gina*, was the one woman he couldn't bear to think would do that to him. Not her. Not the one woman in the history of his life that he decided he was going to go all-out for. Not the one woman he wanted to get to know better to determine if she could actually become his life partner.

And the thought of it, that he was so busy trying not to play her while he himself might have been getting played, shocked him. And angered him.

But mostly it just hurt him.

Unable to deal with such new, highly-charged feelings, he turned away from the window and went to his bar. He poured himself a big drink even though it was very early in the morning. But he needed something to stop the pain. He needed something to remind him that he was being irrational and that a man like him could not possibly care that some woman left him high and dry.

But just as he took his first swallow of alcohol, her beautiful brown face flashed before him. And those big, alluring eyes. And that beautiful white smile and happy laugh. And the way they made love together.

And it still hurt. He couldn't lie and pretend it didn't. It hurt! Some female he had managed to spend all of one night with was distressing him already. And if she could have him this discombobulated already, what in the world did that say about the future of his heart? She'd run roughshod over it, if he wasn't careful.

But it wasn't as if he didn't deserve to lose her before he even had her, he thought. The way he'd run roughshod over so many other women and their hearts, he deserved it and so much more. But that didn't make it hurt any less.

Because it still hurt.

Because Karma was still a bitch. And for Gentleman James, it was called Gina that morning.

CHAPTER SEVENTEEN

Tamira and Kim were both still asleep by the time Gina arrived home. And it was a good thing, too, because all she could think to do was hurry to her room, close the door, and cry some more.

Why didn't she remember him before it went this far? But she knew why. It had been fifteen years! How could she have remembered him? She didn't make love to him thinking she would get pregnant by him. She didn't make love to him thinking he would become the father of her child. She saw him the way he saw her: as a one-night-stand at a party neither one of them found interesting. It wasn't a life decision. It was a why not. It was a *let's have some fun* moment when she knew even then she should have never been that cavalier about sleeping with a man she'd just met.

But she was young and dumb and a little sex starved too. And he was gorgeous and more than willing to give her what she needed. He knew how to activate her hormones, and she apparently knew how to activate his. And that was the beginning and end of it for both of them.

Or so they thought.

Gina fell on her bed and stared up at the ceiling. A night that had started out so promising ended up worst than she could have ever imagined it would. Because her secret was out in the open now. A secret that could turn Tamira against her even more than she already was. She thought she was doing her daughter a favor. Don't miss what you cannot have. That was why she said her father was dead. She had to cut off any talk of him in its tracks because she knew nothing to tell her. He had obviously given her a fake name, so she didn't even know his name, and it was all just so sordid! And her daughter's future stood in the balance.

She turned over, hoping to dismiss any thoughts of James Serrano. But she failed miserably. All she thought about, when she wasn't thinking about Tamira, was James.

But then her daughter was pounding on her bedroom door. "You up, Ma? I can't be late. I have a presentation in first period."

"I'll be ready!" Gina called out, and then got up and got herself in the shower. And once in there, she was crying again.

But by the time she made it into the kitchen, with Tam ready to go, she had her act together. At least on the surface. "Where's

Kim?" she asked her daughter.

"She just left. She said she'll see you at the office."

Gina made herself a cup of coffee.

"I'm going to the library after school," Tamira said.

"I'll pick you up," said Gina.

"Ma! I'm going with friends."

"I'll pick them up too."

"But why? I'm no little kid. I'm fifteen years old!"

"That's why," said Gina. "You're fifteen."

Then Gina was just tired of fighting. Her whole life seemed to be one big fight. "Let's go," she said, as she poured her remaining coffee down the drain.

Tamira was upset as she grabbed her bookbag and headed out of the backdoor that led to the garage as her mother was grabbing her own briefcase.

"And don't you dare slam my door either," she warned her upset daughter.

But Tamira was already in the process of slamming it, and it slammed shut.

Gina, angry, hurried to that door, opened it, and then hurried up to her daughter. She turned her around angrily. "Get your ass back inside that house and close that door like you've got some sense! I'm not playing with you, little girl!"

Even Tamira could see how angry her mother was. It seemed almost out of place for just slamming a door. She was always slamming doors. What was the big deal?

But Tamira also knew not to sass her mother when she was in that mood. And she definitely was in a very bad mood that morning. So she did as she was ordered. She went back and opened the door, and then properly closed it.

Gina was satisfied, but it wasn't showing on her face. She looked bewildered to Tamira, as if something was going on internally with her mother that she couldn't reconcile. And it worried Tamira. So much so that she went over to her mother and hugged her.

Gina, always surprised when the real Tamira Griffin came through, hugged her back vigorously. And tears appeared in her eyes again.

Tamira saw those tears when they stopped embracing. "What's wrong, Ma?" she asked her.

But Gina was shaking her head. "Just good to see my baby back," she said, and Tamira smiled.

But as they piled into Gina's Camry, and Tamira kept looking at her mother, she knew something more was going on than what her mother had said. And she began to wonder if it had something to do with her date last night. Did it go all wrong, or all right? Her mother would be upset if it had gone wrong, because it would be just like all those other dates before him. But she would be upset, too, had it gone all right because she would be so unaccustomed to good fortune that she would squander it. Either way, it wouldn't bode well for her mother, and Tamira knew it.

She took her mother's hand as she drove her to school, and squeezed it.

CHAPTER EIGHTEEN

When Gina arrived at her office, the last thing she expected to find was a full-scale revolt. But that was exactly what she had on her hands. A revolt. From her clients in the factory case.

"They're waiting for you," Kim said as Gina entered her storefront office.

"Who's waiting?"

"Roosevelt and gang," said Kim. "I had to put them in the conference room. They came with anger in their souls."

"Over what?"

"They won't tell me. They want you. You're the object of their hatred."

Gina shook her head. "All I need," she said as she walked with her briefcase to the conference room just adjacent to the waiting room. And as soon as she opened the door and made her way up to the head of the table, they let her have it.

"How could you betray us this way?" asked Roosevelt, their leader. It was ten of them. And all of them, like Kim said, had tongues loaded for bear.

"How have I betrayed you, Mr. Roosevelt?" Gina responded.

"You turned down a year's salary?" Roosevelt asked this with the same shock in his voice he had when he first heard the news.

Gina was surprised that they even knew about that offer that was long since off the table, and that they would be upset about it considering the millions they were actually suing for.

"You do understand that that would be pennies compared to what you could get."

"But we ain't got nothing!" said another one of the workers. "And we got bills to pay."

"Do you realize how far a year's wages could have taken us?" asked Roosevelt. "I wouldn't be losing my house if I had that money in my pocket right now!"

"It would not have happened that fast," said Gina.

"But it would have happened!" yelled Roosevelt. "But you went and turned it down behind our backs. Now we got nothing!"

"There's something," Gina said. "I made a counteroffer."

This interested all of them. "What kind of counteroffer?" Roosevelt asked.

"Two-hundred-and-fifty-thousand dollars apiece, plus five years of company health insurance. And I also asked for payment within five days of acceptance."

Everybody was excited. "They agreed to that?" Roosevelt asked doubtfully.

Gina exhaled. "Not yet, no," she said, and the room was deflated again. "But they're considering it."

"That ain't good enough!" Roosevelt yelled. "That other lawyer, who told us what you were up to, says you're an embarrassment to the profession for not taking that deal. He said it's the best deal we're likely to ever get."

"And you turned it down!" said another one, and the recriminations started anew.

In the waiting room at her desk out front, Kim was listening to the craziness. But she knew Gina had a plan if they'd only let her implement it. The fact that Serrano was considering the offer was normal practice, and she could hear Gina trying to tell them that. But their minds were made up. They wanted out and this was as good a reason as any.

And then Kim noticed that Mercedes-Maybach pull up into the parking lot, and she saw James Serrano getting out.

She wanted to hurry in and tell Gina that she had company, and to pipe it down, but he was inside the office before she could get from behind her desk. So she stayed put.

"May I help you?" she asked as he

walked up to her desk.

James was already hearing commotion coming from that closed door just off from the waiting room, and that consumed his attention. Was Gina alright?

"May I help you?" Kim asked again.

"Yes, I'm looking for Miss Griffin."

"She's not available right now, but you're welcome to wait. May I ask who's here to see her?"

James was surprised that she didn't remember him from his visit to that office last week. "Jim Serrano," he said.

"Yes, sir. You may have a seat and she'll be right with you."

But almost as if on cue, the conference door flew open and Roosevelt and company were hurrying out.

"A disgrace, that's what he said," said Roosevelt. "An embarrassment to the profession."

"You're making a mistake, Mr. Roosevelt," said Gina, coming out too.

"The only mistake we made was hiring you!" Roosevelt shot back.

"The least you could have done was give us a chance to turn down that offer," Harriett said. "But you didn't even do that."

"She thinks she knows better than we

do," said Roosevelt. "Now we're taking charge of this. And you're fired!" he said with fire on his tongue and nobody, this time, tried to defend Gina. She looked flustered to James as they all headed out of the office as she let them go.

James continued to stare at her. Why was his heart fluttering just looking at her? "What was that about?" he asked her.

But Gina just stood there, rubbing her forehead. She was beyond flustered, he thought. And he couldn't help it. His heart was breaking for her. He went over to her and pulled her into his arms.

Gina would have fought him. Why was he even there? She couldn't deal with him right now! But she needed him. She needed that warm feeling she felt in his arms. And she didn't resist. She didn't think she could.

When they stopped embracing, James looked at her. "Are those your factory clients?"

Gina nodded. "Yes."

"And they're upset why?"

"I didn't tell them about your firm's settlement offer."

"I haven't accepted it yet."

"Not that offer. The first one. The one with the year's wages."

James hesitated. She should have told her clients before she let her emotions take over and she turned it down flat, but that was her inexperience. "That offer's off the table," he said.

"I tried to tell them that, but that only made them more determined to get rid of me."

James exhaled. "Here's what I'll do. I'll go to those motherfuckers and tell them they can get any attorney they want, but all settlement offers are off the table, including the latest one you submitted. See if they get a penny out of me."

But Gina was already shaking her head. "No, James, you can't," she said with a plea in her voice. "No. Please. Don't do that to them. They're just trying to survive, and I should have realized that. Because they're right. I should have told them about that offer. I knew I could get more for them, but they need whatever they can get. But it's too late now."

"Not if he goes on and accept your offer," said Kim, and both James and Gina looked at her.

"I'm just saying," she added, looking away.

Gina waited for James to say so. She knew he probably had the power to accept it on the spot. But he didn't. Just the opposite. "That offer's been rejected," he said bluntly. "They get a new attorney, and we'll deal with that attorney.

But I already decided we were taking it to court. And with the kind of people I'll have on that jury, they'll never see a dime. And it'll serve them right."

Kim and Gina both were horrified by his cutthroat attitude. It was as if he didn't understand what poor people went through at all!

"Can I talk with you in my office?" Gina asked James.

James knew he wasn't going to change his mind, but he also knew he had something else on his mind. Something that was so beyond that case she wanted to talk to him about, that even he didn't quite know how to handle the discussion. He just knew they needed to have one.

"Yes," he said.

But before she could escort him to her office, Mae, one of her factory clients, came back into the building.

"What is it, Mae?" Gina asked her.

"Don't you never mind, Roosevelt. We gonna give you another week to see if they accept your new offer before we sign any papers with that new firm. And if me and Harriett don't sign, since we're the original filers, there will be no new representation. You're still our lawyer, until you find out if the accepted your offer or not."

Gina knew James had already turned it down, and was about to tell her so, but Kim interrupted her.

"Thank you, Mae. We'll call y'all as soon as we hear something."

Mae smiled, satisfied, and hurried back out of the office.

Gina looked at Kim. "He turned it down," she said.

"They gave us some time," said Kim. "Maybe we'll come up with something else. Okay?"

Gina just wanted to go crawl under a rock somewhere and stay there. She was over it. But that was why she was glad she had Kim. She was in no state to make any decisions that morning. "Okay," she said, and then she escorted James to her office.

CHAPTER NINETEEN

He closed the door behind them and sat in front of her desk. She sat behind her desk.

"How can I help you?" James asked, folding his legs.

He had showered and shaved and was in another one of those tailored suits he loved to wear, Gina could tell. And even in her distress she was getting flashbacks in her head about that wonderful night they spent together. It seemed so hopeful. Until she saw that tattoo. "I thought you were going to let your client review my counter," she said.

"I have. It was rejected."

She had hoped he would accept her proposal and she could hurry and tell her clients. "You've presented it to Donovan already?"

"It was rejected," James said again.

"You told me that already." Then Gina stared at him. "Sounds like you rejected it."

"I give my advice. Unlike those ungrateful pricks for clients you have, my client takes my advice," he said.

Gina didn't know what to make of James. He seemed unnecessarily harsh this morning. He seemed nothing like the gentleman she was with last night. He seemed almost as if he was so pissed-off he could hardly contain his rage, and it had nothing to do with her clients. "What is it, James?" she asked him.

James knew his anger wasn't about those clients either. It was about *her*. He looked at her. "Why did you leave me?" he asked her.

"I needed to."

"You could have awakened me."

"You were sleeping so peacefully I didn't see the point."

James frowned. "You didn't see the point? Are you fucking kidding me?"

"You can drop the language," Gina said firmly.

"Fuck the language!" James spat out. "You weren't worrying about the language when I was fucking your brains out last night!"

Gina was shocked that he would have gone there. She stood up quickly. "Don't you dare talk to me like that!"

James was upset with himself, too, for letting his *other* side come out so forcefully. When it wasn't anger at all that was driving it. He was just hurt. "I apologize for that," he said to her. "I didn't mean to--"

"You'd better go," said Gina. She didn't want to hear it.

But James remained seated. Because

there was something still bothering him. Something they didn't address last night at all. "You called me Ross," he said.

Gina's heart dropped. Did she slip up and say that name while they were making love? But how could she? She didn't even realize who he was while they were making love!

James saw the changed look on her face. He had hit a nerve. His suspicion, that she had once upon a time been one of his one-night conquests, was spot on. "You called me Ross in that parking lot at Donovan's office," he said.

Gina was at least relieved that she hadn't subconsciously called the man the only name she knew him as fifteen years ago. And she sat back down.

"I had planned to ask about it this morning when we woke up. But your unceremonious decampment put a halt to that." Then he looked her straight in the eyes. "We slept together before last night, Gina. Didn't we?"

Gina's big eyes wanted to fill with tears, but she fought back all emotions. "Yes," she said. "We did. I realized it for certain when I saw your arrow tattoo."

James let out a long exhale. "Where did it happen? How long ago? I would have remembered you."

But Gina was shaking her head. "No, you wouldn't have. It wasn't recent," she said.

"How long ago?"

Gina didn't want to say. She didn't want to expose any more than she had to expose. She'd withheld information all those years, but she never lied. She wasn't about to start now. "Fifteen years ago," she said.

"Whoa," said James. "No wonder I didn't remember you! That was a lifetime ago."

"And so many women ago?" Gina asked him.

He didn't hesitate. "Yes," he said. "Unfortunately. Where were we?"

"At a party. A frat party in Latham, where I went to school."

"Latham?" James asked. And suddenly he remembered. It was easy to remember! Fifteen years ago, he was a practicing attorney, and had been one for several years. But his kid brother Vinny was in college at that time and because there was some threat to the Serrano crime family, James was tasked with babysitting Vinny at his wild frat party that night. And it was in Latham, Illinois. It was the last time he had been in that town, not by design, but because that same night somebody shot Vinny and Carmine, mortified, ordered both brothers back to Chicago.

He also remembered there was a girl there that he fucked.

He looked at Gina. "That was you?" he asked her, still stunned.

Gina hesitated. But then she answered honestly. "Yes," she said. "A kid had been shot with a pellet gun."

It was a real gun, and that kid was James's kid brother Vinny. "I remember you," James said now that that night was clear in his memory. "You were the one with all the questions."

Normally, Gina would have smiled. She always was inquisitive. But she was too distressed for smiling.

"My condom broke that night," he said. "It was the first and last time that ever happened to me. And that was you?"

"Although you told me last night you never had sex without a condom."

"I never did! It broke, but I had one on! And that was you?"

Gina nodded. "That was me, yes."

But James was still puzzled. "When did you realize it was me?" he asked her. "Was it in that parking lot when you called me Ross?"

"I had a suspicion that you somehow reminded me of him, but then it didn't add up.

Your name wasn't Ross. It was James. And I assumed you had at some point attended Bayard, but I looked you up and you never did."

"I hate to admit it," James said, "but Ross was the name I used to have my cake and eat it too. I wanted as small a footprint as I could manage."

"So that ladies wouldn't be able to trace the heartbreaker?" Gina asked him.

James stared at her. "I broke your heart?"

"No!" she said firmly. "I knew what that night was about, and it had nothing to do with neither one of our hearts. But. . ." She just couldn't bring herself to say it.

"But what?" James asked.

"But you left an impression," was the best Gina could muster.

James unfolded his legs and leaned forward. He rested his arms on his muscular thighs. "I wish I can say the same thing," he said.

Gina wondered if he'd just insulted her, but he quickly explained.

"It has nothing to do with you," he explained. "I'm amazed, frankly, that I didn't remember you. But I had so many women I couldn't keep track of them from one day to the next. I was sleeping my way through life back then."

"Back then?" Gina asked him.

"You're right," he said. "Still." Then he decided to go there. "Until last night."

Gina knew that was probably another one of his lines, but it still resonated with her. But will he still be interested when he found out the truth?

Gina's office door opened before either of them could speak another word, and Kim rushed in. "It's the hospital, Gina." She sounded out of breath.

"Is my daughter alright?" Gina asked nervously.

"They wouldn't tell me what it's about," Kim said, and Gina quickly picked up her desk phone.

But James was surprised. "Daughter?" he said out loud. "You have a daughter?"

But Gina had already pressed the blinking button and was answering the call. "Hello?"

"Is this Ms. Griffin?"

"Yes, may I help you?"

"Are you the mother of Tamira Griffin?"

Gina's heart dropped. It was about her daughter! "Yes," said. "What's happened? Is she alright?"

"I'm the nurse at Baptist Medical here in

Chicago. Your daughter, I'm afraid, has been in a serious car accident."

Gina jumped to her feet. "A car crash?" she asked. James stood up too, and Kim hurried to the desk, with one hand over her heart. "Is she alright?" Gina asked, nervously holding the phone with both hands.

"I wanted to make sure I had the correct parent," said the nurse on the phone.

But Gina didn't care about that. She was about to jump out of her skin and that lady was talking about something that she didn't give a shit about. "Just tell me if my daughter's alright. Please tell me she's alright!"

"She's alright," the nurse said quickly. "She's okay."

Gina settled back down.

"She's alright?" Kim asked her.

"Yes," said Gina. "But how could she be in a car accident?" Gina asked the nurse. "She's at school. I dropped her off myself."

"It's not a matter to discuss over the phone. Could you come?"

"Of course. I'm on my way!"

The nurse told her which floor, and then Gina ended the call and began hurrying from around her desk.

"Did she say what happened?" Kim asked.

"No," said Gina. "I've got to get there. I've got to see for myself that she's okay."

James could feel her pain because it was that palpable. "I'll drive you," he said and immediately placed his hand on her back as they made their way toward the front.

"I'll hold things down here," said Kim, following them. "But you keep me posted, GG."

"I will," said Gina, looking back at Kim, whom she knew loved Tamira too. And then she and James hurried out of the office, got into his Mercedes, and took off.

Kim stood at the window and watched. They got fired and now this. Sweet Tamira might be injured. Their beloved Tamira. It was turning out to be a horrible day.

CHAPTER TWENTY

The drive to the hospital was quiet even though James was speeding through the streets like a madman and Gina wasn't mad at him for doing so. She wanted to get to that hospital so badly she could taste her fear. Because her child was involved. Because her child had been in some car crash when she was supposed to be in school. Gina rubbed her forehead. She was failing on every front!

James looked over at her when they pulled up to a red light. He could not only see her distress, but this time he could feel it too. "Don't worry yourself to death, Gina," he said to her.

"Too late for that," said Gina.

James glanced at her again. "How old is she?" he asked her.

Gina wasn't thinking about the timeline or the fact that he was her father or any of that. That was why she answered without thinking. "Fifteen," she said.

"Ah. She's in the terrible teens," he said.

"And then some," said Gina.

But then James thought again. Fifteen. That would mean Gina, who was now thirty-three, had her daughter when she was eighteen. Which meant she got pregnant with her daughter when she was a freshman at Bayard!

He looked at her. But it couldn't be! It just couldn't be!

He was about to say something, but the cars behind him began honking their horns. The light had changed.

He looked through the rearview, and then looked at the light, and he took off.

And he didn't have the nerve to say another word.

They arrived at Baptist Medical, were fortunate to find a parking spot right near the entrance, and Gina jumped out running toward the entrance before James could get out of his car good. By the time he had hurried inside, she was already getting on the elevator. He got in just as the door was about to close her in.

Once the doors closed, he looked at her. "Gina," he said, "you've got to pull yourself together. Don't let your daughter see you in this state."

Gina knew he spoke the truth. She was going mad with worry. "I just need to see her," she said. "I just need to make sure she's okay. Then I'll be okay."

James hesitated. But he knew he had to

say it. "Where's her father?" he asked.

A tear that was already settled in Gina's eye, began to roll down her pretty face. Another terrible mistake she made in her life! Another terrible decision she made that didn't just affect her, but her daughter and her daughter's father too.

James moved over to her, and he wiped her tear away. She looked up at him. And he looked at her. And no words had to be spoken. Still too terrifying for him to even think it, he pulled her into his arms as they quietly traveled up to the seventh floor.

When they got up to the pediatric ward, several parents were already there, and police officers. And one of the parents was crying hysterically. The others were trying to comfort her, but she refused to be comforted. Gina and James hurried to the nurse's station.

"Where's my daughter?"

"Your name?"

"Gina Griffin. Her name is Tamira Griffin."

"Oh," said the nurse as if she had suddenly lost all sympathy. "This way," she said with ice in her voice, and then she escorted Gina and James further down the hospital hallway to a room. And then she just left them there.

James and Gina looked at each other.

What was that about, they wondered. But they didn't wonder long. James opened the door, and they walked on in.

When they first entered the room, Gina was shocked. Her daughter was in that room with two men who appeared to be interrogating her. But she was in tears, and she had on handcuffs!

Even as Gina hurried to her biracial daughter, James stopped in his tracks as soon as he saw Tamira. Because she looked so familiar. Because she reminded him of his kid brother Vinny, when he was a child. His heart dropped through his shoe.

But Gina was laser focused on her daughter. "What in the world is going on here?" she asked, hurrying to Tamira. "Why is my child in handcuffs?"

"Mommy, make them stop!" cried Tamira. "I told them it's not true!"

"What's not true?" Gina, the mother, quickly asked.

But James, the attorney, stopped Tamira from answering. "Don't say anything," he regained his bearings and said to the child. He hurried to her too.

"And who are you supposed to be?" one of the men, a plainclothes detective, asked him.

"I'm her attorney," James said. "Jim

Serrano. And she has nothing further to say."

"But what is this about?" Gina asked the detectives. "And who are you?"

"Are you her mother?"

"Yes! Who are you?"

"I'm Detective Raines and that's Detective Philpot. We're with Robbery/Homicide."

Gina and James both frowned. "Robbery/Homicide?" asked Gina. "But I was told my child was in a car crash."

"She was. And she was the driver of that car."

"That's not true!" Tamira cried.

James moved next to her. "Not another word," he said to her with stress in his voice. But when he saw the pain in her beautiful eyes, he nearly broke himself. But he knew he had to maintain because Gina was already broken.

"Are you saying my daughter drove the getaway car?" Gina asked the detective.

"No ma'am. There was no robbery. They were just out joyriding. And your daughter was driving."

"She said she wasn't."

"According to every child that was in that car with her, except one, she was the driver. She was the one who ran into that truck."

Gina and James both felt as if they were

going to die. "What truck?" James asked.

"The one she crashed into," said Detective Raines. "The one that killed Tonya Redding."

"Oh God no!" Gina cried out, and looked at Tamira.

"Tonya's dead, Ma!" Tamira said, still crying too. "She's dead!"

Gina pulled her daughter into her arms again and couldn't help but let the tears flow from her eyes too. She'd known Tonya for years. She could hardly believe she was gone. That apparently was her mother out front, the mother Gina had never seen, who was crying so hysterically.

James placed his arms on the backs of both women. It took all he had not to break down too. These children! Now one was gone, and one was being charged with what? Her *murder*?

James looked at the detectives. "Is she under arrest?"

"You bet cha," said Raines.

"What's the charge?" James asked, and Gina looked too.

"Vehicular homicide," said Raines.

"Good Lord," Gina said, her face unable to hide her anguish.

"How on earth could you even attempt to

charge this child with VH?"

"She was the driver," Raines said.

But James cut him off. "She said she wasn't!"

"Every child in that car with her, except for Tonya Redding, who can't speak anymore unfortunately, said she was. That's all we need to effect an arrest."

Gina and James knew it too. And Gina knew, in that instant, their lives would never be the same again. She also knew she had to prepare her daughter for that eventuality too. She stopped embracing her child and placed her hands on either side of Tamira's beautiful face. "Listen to me," she said. "Are you listening?"

Tamira was still crying, but she nodded her head.

"They will take you into custody," Gina said. "But know that I'll be working . . ." She looked at James, who looked devastated too, whose legal prowess far exceeded hers. And she needed that prowess for their child's sake. "*We'll* be working to make certain you get out, okay?"

"Okay," Tamira said like the kid she was.

"And no matter what somebody ask you," Gina continued, "do not discuss this case. Not to the Police. Not to the other girls who will be in that cell with you. Not to anybody. I don't care if they claim to be your attorney. They aren't. Nobody's representing you but James and I, okay? We're the only two people you say a word to, and only after we tell you to say so. Understand me, Tam?"

Tamira nodded. "Yes, ma'am," she said.

And Gina saw the regret all over her. All those times she didn't listen. All those times she thought Gina was being overly harsh. Now she knew better. Gina only prayed it wasn't too late for her the way it was for Tonya.

She held onto James and, in truth, James held onto her, as two policemen took their child away.

And Gina couldn't bear it. She couldn't bear letting her baby out of her sight. She, with James still holding onto her, followed Tamira and the officers detaining her as they left the room, went out into the corridor, and began heading toward the elevators. But the problem were the parents. They had to walk by those parents first.

James immediately knew that was a bad idea. With such high emotions in that hallway, why didn't those cops find a back way to take that child? Were they this callous, even with a child?

They apparently were because as soon

as Tamira, still in handcuffs, still in the grasp of those police officers, began to approach those parents, they saw her coming and ran to her. When they started screaming at her as if they were yelling at a full-grown adult, James and Gina sprang into action, too, hurrying to Tamira.

But not before those policemen allowed parents to spit on Tamira and continue to scream at her, and they even allowed one of the parents to slap Tamira before James was able to pull him away from her and throw him to the ground. He wanted to kick his ass, too, but he had to stave off those other angry parents because the cops weren't doing a damn thing. It was Gina, not those cops, who made herself a human shield in front of her daughter, protecting her while James protected them.

But it would take the two detectives running out of the room to gain any semblance of control of those rowdy, volatile, pain-stricken parents.

"Go the back way!" Detective Raines yelled at the uniformed officers and they hurried the back way with Tamira even as the parents were still screaming at her and still trying to get to her. But they couldn't get beyond where those two detectives stood.

James and Gina hurried with Tamira and the officers. They were going to make sure no other incident happened while they were still able to be around her. And when they all got on a back elevator, Gina was livid. "Why didn't you bring her this way to begin with?" Gina angrily asked those police officers. "You knew those parents were out there!"

"She killed that child," said one of the officers. "How did you expect them to react?"

But Gina fired back. "First of all, she didn't kill anybody. Get your shit straight, alright? And second of all, that's why you should have known better than to take my child anywhere near them! You knew what would happen!" Gina was up in one of those officers faces. "You knew what would happen!"

"Gina," James said, pulling her back just as that officer placed his hand on the gun in his holster.

Gina backed off then. And looked at her daughter with such anguish on her face that Tamira was more worried about Gina! She'd never seen her mother quite that unhinged. "I'm alright, Ma," she said to her, to reassure her, and James stared at Tamira. "Just calm down please. Don't be worried like this. I'm okay."

James held Gina tightly as a reminder that he had warned her against showing her devastation to her daughter. It would impact Tamira, and it apparently had.

Gina, remembering that warning, tried to get it back together, for Tamira's sake. "We'll get you out of this, Tam," she said instead, attempting to reignite hope in a hopeless situation. "We'll work around the clock to get you out of this situation."

Tamira looked at James. James was already staring at her. "He said he's my lawyer," Tamira said.

Gina looked at James. Were those just words he was saying earlier, or did he really intend to fight for their child?

James nodded. "Yes, I'm your attorney," he said. "My name is Jim Serrano. Your mother and I will get you out of this situation, I promise you. But you do not discuss your case with anybody, not even a cell mate like your mother said. Okay?"

Tamira nodded. But she found herself staring at James even as he was staring at her.

For James, he felt his heartstrings pull toward that child.

For Tamira, she felt as if she were looking at somebody she knew, although she didn't think she'd ever seen him before in her life.

But the situation was crazy enough and her emotions were too raw for her to feel as if it was all just so murky. She looked away from

James.

And the elevator door opened, and they all stepped off.

When they made it around the side of the building to the patrol car, the officer did allow Gina to give her daughter a hug. "We'll get you out of there as quickly as we can, okay?" Gina said, refusing to let that officer's power play get to her.

Tamira nodded. And the tears returned. "Tonya died, Ma," she said, as if all she could think about wasn't her own freedom, but her friend's death. That sentiment, that she wasn't a selfish teen, wasn't lost on James.

Gina took her hand and placed it on the side of Tamira's pretty face. "She's in a better place, baby. Don't you worry about Tonya, okay? She's alright. I want you to concentrate on doing what Mr. James told you to do. If anybody tries to interrogate you, or if some other prisoner asks you questions about what happened, you keep your mouth shut. They will twist it around and use it against you. Even if they threaten to harm you, which they'd better not," Gina added, glancing at those cops, "you do not say a word. Mr. James and I are both lawyers," she said, to remind those cops to watch themselves, "and we'll get you out of this just like we promised. Okay?"

227

Tamira nodded. "Okay, Mommy," she said, and when she called her that name she only called her when she was happy or in great distress, Gina's heart broke all over again.

And they placed Tamira in the backseat of that patrol car, got in themselves, and appeared to be doing paperwork rather than driving off.

Gina was so focused on staring at her daughter, and waving at her, and mouthing that she was going to be alright, that she didn't realize James had left her side. Until she saw him driving up behind the patrol car. She got into his car.

"We'll follow that patrol car to juvenile detention," he said, "and then we'll get busy."

"Where do we start?" Gina asked as James leaned over toward her seatbelt.

"We've got to get her out of there first," he said, putting the seatbelt around Gina.

"And then what?" Gina asked.

"And then we work on getting those charges dropped," James said, leaning back up and stopping when he and Gina were face to face and so close that their noses were almost touching. And his heart began to flutter.

He made a hasty decision last night that he was going to see where a relationship with Gina would lead, but now it didn't seem hasty at all. He felt connected to Gina in a way he'd never felt connected before. And it wasn't just because they slept together before. It wasn't even just because of what he suspected was true but had to be confirmed. It was because of Gina. It was because, every once in a lifetime, you find your soul mate. You find somebody who made you feel and act and believe unlike anybody else ever had. That was what James was feeling for Gina.

And he closed his eyes and kissed her gently on the lips. Gina found herself closing her eyes too. Because that simple kiss felt like a reassurance. And then he opened his eyes and said the words she could only dream a man would say to her. "I'll never leave you, Gina," James said to her. "No matter what comes our way, I'll never leave you."

Gina's heart squeezed with emotion when he said those words. Because they could not have been said at a better moment in time. Because it was at the worst moment, the lowest point, of Gina's life. Her baby was in a patrol car right in front of her, accusing of killing another baby. She was now a statistic in the worst possible way, something Gina had worked Tamira's whole life to never let happen. She thought she was working to keep her daughter from having a baby out of wedlock, or from getting on drugs. But this was beyond anything she could have ever imagined! A joyride? A wreck? A *death*?

But they now had James in their corner. And he promised to stick by them. And the oddest thing about it to Gina, since she never believed a word all those smooth-joe men would tell her down through the years, was that she believed James. She believed him.

And the tears she didn't want to come, came. "Thank you," she said to him so heartfelt that he felt it too. And hugged her.

They stayed hugged up together, knowing as attorneys that Tamira was about to face a long, uphill climb, until that patrol car began to move. And they moved right along with it.

CHAPTER TWENTY-ONE

After following the officers to that detention center, and after going inside to make sure Tamira was still okay after transport, they knew there was nothing more they could do in that moment. She was being processed in. It could take three or four hours they were told, but they still didn't leave. They remained in the area. Because she was a juvenile, they would either release her to her mother, or allow her to be released on bond. They were prepared for either eventuality. They did not want to even entertain the no bond scenario. But as attorneys of record for Tamira, they had a right to see her before that hearing.

But in the meantime, they went next door to the diner, and ordered two cups of coffee.

And they drank it, at a window booth, in silence.

James kept taking peeps at Gina. He knew he was going to have to put his practice on hold, and perhaps his entire life on hold until they had Tamira's case thrown out. And it stunned him that he didn't find it strange. He was no altruistic man in the main. He was, by and large, selfish and self-centered. But something about Gina had him going for broke. This was either going to be the best decision of his life, or the worst he could have ever made. There would be no in-between. He was past forty now. Being alone all his life wasn't comforting anymore. And it was Gina he wanted. Nobody else. He was going to do everything in his power to make this work.

He kept taking peeps at Gina as he drank his coffee, wondering why did he choose her to make it work?

Gina was mostly looking at her coffee. She barely touched it. She kept thinking about everything, but that hospital scene still shocked her. The mood of the other parents inside that hospital was filled with so much tension that even she felt threatened by their anger and hatred. Tamira, they decided, was the enemy. Little Tamira, they decided, was the only one responsible and their innocent sweet babies didn't have shit to do with it. They were just going along for the ride, let those parents tell it. Gina and James both knew that was the line they were going to take. Gina and James both knew over their dead bodies they were going to get away with it.

But they first had something to discuss themselves.

And as they sat in that diner waiting for

Tamira to be processed in, Gina knew it was now or never. Her face was frowned, and serious. It was as if her whole world was crashing in all around her, and she needed an off ramp. "When that condom broke," she said to James, "I ended up pregnant."

She looked at him, although she was reasonably certain he already knew it by now. But she had to say it. It was on her to speak the words. "I ended up pregnant with my . . . with *our* daughter," she said.

James didn't say anything at first. His eyes remained glued to the road outside of the window. His hands were glued onto that coffee cup. His body remained so stiff and tight it would pop had it been a balloon.

"What I'm trying to say," Gina started saying, because he didn't seem to get the full impact of what she meant.

But he got it. He knew that confirmation would come. "I know what you're saying," he said to her. "She's my daughter." He looked at Gina. "That's what you're saying."

Gina nodded. No more tears about that. She had to save them for her child. "That's what I'm saying," she said.

James looked back at the road outside and let out a long, hard exhale. "I knew it the moment I laid eyes on her," he said.

Gina stared at him.

"I had a suspicion she might be mine when we were still at your office; when I found out you had a daughter. And when you told me her age, that only solidified my belief. But when I saw her for myself," he said, shaking his head, "there was no doubt about it. She looks just like my baby brother looked when he was around that age." Then he managed to smile. "He was nothing but trouble back then."

But Gina still couldn't smile. "She's in a world of trouble herself, James. No matter what the truth is, they're going to try to pin it on her. On the black girl. The only person of color that was in that group."

James nodded. "That's exactly what they're angling to do. You've got that right. But don't get this wrong," James added, and looked at Gina. "I won't let that happen."

Tears appeared in Gina's eyes again. "Thank you," she said.

Then he frowned. He had so many questions! "What kind of kid is she, Gina?" he asked her. "Is she good to people and smart and--"

"Yes," said Gina, nodding her head. "Oh, yes. She's very good to people. She has a big heart, James. A really big heart. And she's smart too. Oh my. Way smarter than you or I."

James smiled. "That's good."

"She's in the Honor Society. She's the vice-president. And she volunteers at a nursing home on the weekends. Just for a couple hours. But she does it."

James loved to hear it. "That's wonderful, Gina. For a teenager, that's wonderful."

"But has she been a model child? If that's what you're asking," Gina said, "the answer is an emphatic no. Not at all. It hasn't been easy raising her, even when she was little. But then she turned fifteen and it was as if all hell broke loose. It was as if she decided I didn't know anything about anything and her friends knew better than I would ever know. But I don't blame her friends. She always had that streak of independence in her, even when she was a stubborn little girl who thought she knew as much as I did." Then Gina frowned. "Based on the fact that I raised her and she's in the kind of trouble she's in right now," she said, "maybe she did."

But James reached over and took Gina's hand. "You will not blame yourself in any way, shape, or form for what has happened. She's a typical teen who wanted to hang out with her friends and have some fun. It turned horribly wrong, but they can never foresee that. And they never want to listen to those of us who can."

Gina looked at James. "I wish she would have known you when she was growing up. That would have really helped her."

James believed that too. But he had a question he was hesitating to ask because he didn't want to add to her stress. But it was a question that needed asking. "Did you ever try to find me?" he asked her.

Gina was floored by the question. "Did I try?" she said, her face a mask of worry. "For years I tried. Years! I even went back to that house, after I found out I was pregnant, to ask if they knew where I could find you. But that house had already been sold and the new owners had never heard of anybody named Ross."

"That house belonged to my big brother Carmine."

Gina remembered the name. The *reputed* mob boss Carmine Serrano. Another issue that needed to be addressed! Her daughter's uncle was a mob boss???

"He sold it after Vinny, that's my kid brother, got shot at that party and nearly died," said James.

Gina was surprised. "He was shot? He nearly died?"

James nodded. "It was that touch and

go, yup. It freaked Carmine out and he wanted no more parts of that house or that town. We never went back."

Gina looked at him. "So that was your brother who had gotten shot that night?"

James nodded. They were beyond family secrets now. "Yes," he said.

"Those bouncers, or bodyguards, or whomever they were, told me he had been shot with a pellet gun and was just fine."

"And that was exactly what I ordered them to say to anybody who asked."

"But he wasn't fine?"

"No. Not for months. But thanks to my brother's contacts, we kept it out of the papers. We kept it off the news. And we managed it ourselves."

Gina exhaled. "Wow," she said. Then she looked at James, remembering the question he had asked her. "But yes," she said, "I tried to find you even beyond that house. But all I had to go on was a name that wasn't even your name, and a vague description of a good-looking guy. People thought I was crazy. But I tried to find you for years."

He squeezed her hand again. "I'm sorry I put you through all of that. I just didn't go back to that area."

"Most of my searching was online

because I left that town shortly after I found out I was pregnant too."

He looked at her. "You dropped out of college?"

Gina shook her head. "Dropped out? No. It was more like they kicked me out."

James felt a lump in his throat. "They kicked you out? Just because you were pregnant?"

"Yes! Bayard is a private Christian school, remember? They had a morals clause that every student had to sign that said moral turpitude, as the rule put it, was an offense punishable by expulsion. And they listed examples of moral turpitude. Getting pregnant out of wedlock was at the top of the list."

James frowned. He felt like shit. "I should have been there for you," he said. But he was too busy sleeping his way across America!

"I know you should have been. But had you known, would you have been?" Gina asked, looking at him.

James looked outside again, and then he looked at his coffee. "I would have hoped so. But back then, I was a different person. I was young and arrogant and had an aversion to anything or anybody that would tie me down. But I was humane. I may not have liked that I had messed up, but I don't think I would have

238

abandoned my own kid."

"That's why I think I searched for you so hard," said Gina. "Because I saw something in you that brief time we were together that convinced me you would be there for your child. Maybe not for me, but you'd be there for your child." Then Gina frowned. "It was probably just wishful thinking."

James looked at her. "What did you do after they kicked you out of school?" he asked her.

Gina leaned back. "I went home and had to deal with my parents' displeasure throughout my whole pregnancy. I was an adject failure in their eyes. A statistic, as my father called me. But they still loved me enough to help me through a rough pregnancy. But after the baby was born, I knew I had to get busy. And get out on my own. And I did. I got a job waiting tables, the kind of job I had when I went to Bayard. Then I went to the local community college and got my AA degree. Then I transferred to Chicago State and got my bachelor's degree. Then I won a full scholarship to DePaul for law school. I got my law degree, went back home to Thatches where I figured I could do the most good, and got to work."

"How did you manage with a kid that whole time?" James asked.

"Barely. My best friend Kim, the girl at the office, she came through for me. She had dropped out of school shortly after I was kicked out, but she ended up with nowhere to go after some family problems. She looked me up and asked if she could stay with me until she got back on her feet. So she became my live-in nanny of sorts, although I didn't pay her because I couldn't afford to, and she stayed with the baby while I went to law school. She's been helping me ever since."

"And you've been helping her. You gave her a place to stay and, eventually, a job too. Right?"

Gina nodded. "We help each other," she said.

James looked at her. "You did good, Gina. The deck was stacked against you, but you still came out on top. You did good."

Gina still couldn't find a way to smile, but she appreciated his vote of confidence. But a part of her, a big part, knew it was misplaced. Had she really done *good*, her daughter would have had enough within herself to not go on that joyride to begin with, and would not be sitting in a jail cell in Chicago.

"You haven't told Tamira. Have you?" James asked her.

Gina shook her head. "No. I told her, the

one time she asked, that her father was dead. Which was wrong. But I was so afraid when she asked that I didn't want to admit I was so irresponsible. I didn't want her to try to find you and get her heart broken. I just . . . I took the easy way out."

"No, you didn't. You protected your child. Which was what you were supposed to do."

But Gina knew better than that. She was wrong.

"We'll tell her together," James said, "when that time comes."

"After this is all over," said Gina. "Not before."

James nodded. "Right," he agreed.

Gina leaned her head back and closed her eyes. Just thinking about Tamira and what she was up against made her heart ache. It was a physical pain she couldn't stop. She loved her child more than life itself!

But when she opened her eyes, she saw that James was staring at her in a way that was lustful, but something else too. When she realized what it was, she spoke up. "I don't expect anything from you," she said quickly. "No child support. Nothing like that."

James stared at her.

"I just wanted you to know you have a daughter, and your daughter's in trouble. I just want you to help her get out of this trouble. That's all I want from you."

James was offended. "That's not up to you," he said, and drank more coffee.

Gina realized her blunder. "I offended you. Didn't I? James, I didn't mean it that way. I just saw that look in your eyes."

"What look?"

"The look of alarm. The look of somebody scared to death of a new responsibility. But please understand: Tamira was and will always be my sole responsibility."

"Not anymore she won't," said James. "From here on out she's our responsibility. And," he added, "both of you are my sole responsibility." James looked at her. "You need to understand that."

Gina stared at him. Could this man be for real? She decided to test him. "That wasn't alarm I saw in your eyes?" she asked him point blank.

"Oh, yes," James admitted freely, passing the test. "It was definitely alarm. I'm not saying this is going to be easy for me. We're just starting on this road, and neither one of us knows how it's going to end. But I am going to finish the journey. With you. With Tamira." Then he smiled. "If you guys will have me."

Then he nodded. "What I'm trying to say

is: I've made up my mind, Genevieve."

Gina exhaled. And instead of tears this time, she actually managed a very thin, but real smile. Because she understood what he meant. He was willing to take a chance on her. But was she willing to take a chance on him?

She didn't have to think about that long. Just one more sip of coffee and she knew she would be. Because it would be like a dream come true. She'd be with her daughter's father. Why wouldn't she take that chance? "I've made up my mind too," she said.

And James didn't beat around the bush. His smile was magnetic, and as big as his big, caring eyes. He got up and went to her, and he gave her a big hug.

But then they both thought about Tamira's situation and placed their own happiness back on the shelf again. He sat back down. They both drank their coffees in silence.

CHAPTER TWENTY-TWO

They were placed in the interview room for the attorneys of defendants, and James and Gina felt that sense of dread return as they waited for Tamira.

James felt especially uneven. The idea that he was a father still hadn't sunk in yet, and his daughter didn't even know yet either. How were they going to navigate that?

But before he could ponder it any longer, the doors to the interview room opened, and Tamira was allowed in. The guard that had escorted her in, went back out and closed the door.

Gina and James stood up as Tamira walked up to their table. Gina knew the attorney was not supposed to touch the client, but she broke protocol because that client was her child. And she hurried around that table and hugged Tamira greatly. Tamira hugged her mother with just as much urgency, and James saw that the child's eyes were closed tightly. She was holding up, he decided, but barely.

When they all sat back down, with Gina and James on one side per protocol, and the client on the other side, they got down to business. Gina and James knew they only had a very limited amount of time.

"Tell us what happened, Tamira," James said.

"We decided to meet up before school and hang out some," Tamira said.

"So you didn't have a meeting before school like you told me?" Gina asked.

James could tell Tamira was embarrassed to admit it to her mother, but she was smart enough to know she had to. "No," she said. "I said that so I could get to school early to hang out with my friends."

"Who were these friends?" Gina asked.

"Tonya and two other girls. But I didn't know those boys were going to show up. I thought it would just be us girls."

"Quit lying, Tam," said Gina bluntly, and James looked at Gina. "You knew," Gina added.

Tamira exhaled, all but conceding her mother's comment. And James became upset. "Listen to me," he said, and Tamira looked at him. "You cannot lie to us. You have to tell us the truth, the whole truth, and nothing but the truth so help you God so that we can get you out of this mess. You understand me child? If we're operating from a point of misinformation, there's no way we can be successful. You must tell us the truth. Hold nothing back. Do you hear me?"

Gina didn't like the tone James was using on her child, but she knew it was necessary. Because Tamira would withhold information if it would make her look bad in her mother's eyes. She got that particular trait from her mother.

But James's sharp tone worked. Tamira nodded her head. "Yes, sir," she said.

"Who were the boys?" Gina asked her.

"I don't know their names," said Tamira, and then she watched as James pulled out his cell phone and thumbed through it.

"You don't know their names," Gina said, "but yet you got in a car with them?"

"We were just gonna go over to Starbucks and get something to drink. I was just going for the ride. I think one of the girls had just met them or something. But the oldest one was the driver. His name was Brandon, I remember that. Brandon was the driver. Not me. I don't know why they're lying on me."

"They're trying to save their own skins. That's why."

"Brandon Raglin," said James. "Nineteen

246

years old."

Gina looked at James. "Nineteen? He was *that* old?"

"According to the arrest papers my office was able to download to me," James said, and Tamira began staring at him.

"A nineteen-year-old," said Gina, shaking her head. "And yet they stood up there, every one of them, and claimed my fifteen-year-old child was the driver, and not his old ass. That she was the ringleader!"

"That's exactly what they're claiming," said James. "But don't worry. His ass won't get away with it. They won't get away with it."

Tamira continued to stare at James. Gina noticed her stare. So did James.

"You okay?" Gina asked her.

"Where did you meet?" Tamira asked them.

There was a moment of hesitation. Neither one of them wanted to drop any more news on Tamira. Not until she was out of danger.

"In Latham," Gina said.

"When?"

Gina hesitated again, but answered her. "When I was in college."

Tamira looked at James. "You were in college too?"

"Graduated." James cleared his throat. "I had already graduated," he said.

They could hear the door unlocking and the guard coming in to retrieve Tamira. Their time was up.

Gina placed her hand on Tamira's hand. "We're working around the clock for you, baby," she said. "We'll get you out of here, okay?"

"Okay," Tamira said. She stood up as the guard placed her in handcuffs.

It broke her parents' hearts to see her like that. But they both held back all emotion. For her sake.

"We'll see you at the bail hearing," James said.

Tamira looked at him again. "They'll let me go home then?" she asked him with the sweetest eyes he'd ever seen.

And he decided right then and there that he would never make a promise to her he might not be able to keep. He knew how unjust the justice system could be, especially for people of color. "We hope so," was the best he could manage to say.

"I love you, baby," Gina said, fighting back tears. And then the guard led Tamira out of the interview room.

James looked at Gina. Gina looked at him. He was devastated too.

"What a way to meet your daughter," she said to him. "And it's all my fault!"

James quickly pulled her into his arms. "No it's not," he said to her empathically. "It's not."

When they stopped embracing, he wiped Gina's tears away.

"What now?" she asked him.

"Let's just hope and pray this bail hearing goes smoothly," he said.

But it didn't go smoothly at all.

It was two hours later. James and Gina sat on either side of Tamira at counsel table as the judge gaveled the hearing in session.

"Who's lead counsel?" he asked.

James stood up without hesitation. "I am, Your Honor," he said, buttoning his suitcoat. "James Serrano."

"Then you will be the only one to speak on behalf of the defendant, Mr. Serrano."

"Yes, sir," said James, and sat back down.

The judge then looked over at the prosecution table. "Does the State oppose bail, Miss Finch?" he asked the DA.

Donna Finch stood up. "It does, sir, yes, sir," she said.

Gina and James quickly looked at the

DA. She had to be kidding them!

Even the judge looked at her over his half-moon reading glasses. "And why, Miss Finch?" he asked.

"A girl died due to Tamira Griffin's carelessness. She got behind the wheel of that automobile. She ran into that SUV. Her actions killed that girl, whose parents are now devastated. Other families are crushed. This act of violence has stricken the community. We ask for no bail," DA Finch said, and sat back down.

The Judge looked at James. "Counsel for the Defendant has an objection?"

"Yes, sir," said James and stood back up. "Tragic though this incident definitely is, the State's hyperbolic language doesn't erase the fact that we are not talking about a hardened criminal here, but a fifteen-year-old little girl. She should be released into her mother's custody. That would be justice. This case screams for an immediate release. But if not, then a minimal bail should be set. We'll take either one. But she must be released, Your Honor. Justice demands it," James added, and sat back down.

DA Finch jumped right back up. "Counsel's client wasn't thinking about justice when she plowed into that SUV and killed Tonya

Redding."

James jumped back up. "Your Honor, that was uncalled for!"

The Judge banged his gavel as murmurs were heard in the courtroom's gallery. "That's enough!" he declared. Then he looked at the DA. "Not in my courtroom, Miss Finch," he said.

Then the judge exhaled. "What about the driver of the SUV?" the judge asked.

Finch stood up again. "Out of fear, he fled the scene, sir, after the crash. And we're actively searching for him. But that doesn't exonerate Tamira Griffin in the least. By every account she was the one at fault. She still must pay for the fact that she was the one who hit that SUV, and that she was the one most responsible for her friend's death."

James, surprised that the driver of the SUV had absconded at the scene, was about to stand up to voice his opinion that such evidence was exculpatory in Tamira's favor, but the Judge didn't allow him to respond. He was ready to make his ruling.

And it was as simple as the prosecution made it out to be. "Bail is denied," he said, banged his gavel, and the hearing was over.

Just like that.

Tamira was remanded back into custody.

Just like that.

Tamira started crying when the guards grabbed her again. "Mommy!" she cried to Gina. "Mommy!"

James's heart broke when he saw her crying again. How could the judge not see that she was just an innocent child who hooked up with the wrong crowd? He held onto Tamira's fragile arm, but the guards pulled her away from him too.

"It's going to be alright, Tam," Gina was saying, fighting back tears. "We'll get you out of this. It's going to be alright!"

But as they took their child away, for the first time Gina nor James felt certain that it was true. They weren't at all sure anymore if they would get her out of this.

And that realization stunned them to their core.

CHAPTER TWENTY-THREE

Silence rode with them in the car as James drove them away from the Chicago courthouse. But when James turned a corner she knew did not lead them back to Thatches, she looked at him. "You don't turn here," she said. "At least not to get to my house."

"We aren't going to your house," said James.

"Then where are we going?"

James hesitated. "This is no time to be idealistic," he said.

Gina frowned. "Who's being idealistic?"

"This is no time to take the high ground."

Gina stared at him. "James, what are you trying to say?"

"Our child is in trouble. A child I intend to get to know. But you heard the DA. They're going hard on this case. You saw those parents at the hospital. You heard the accusations hurled at you when the police had to intervene and escort us out of there. All they see is this bad black kid troublemaker who influenced their good little innocent white kids and caused everything to happen, including the death of that girl."

"Innocent my ass," said Gina.

"You know it and I know it and guess what?" asked James. "They know it too."

"And a bad kid and troublemaker?" Gina asked. "That don't even sound like Tam!"

"It's not her," said James. "I've only seen her twice and even I can see that. But that's the picture they prefer to believe, and that's the picture they intend to paint of her. You're an attorney just as I am. We both know how unjust our criminal *justice* system can be. Especially for minorities." He looked at Gina. "We need help."

Gina stared at him. "Your brother?" she asked him.

He exhaled. "I'm afraid so, Gina. Nobody has the contacts he has. Nobody has the reach and pull and power he has. At least nobody I know. We need him to pull out the stops for Tamira."

Gina leaned her head back against the leather headrest, and she felt as if she was drowning. She felt as if she was flailing in the middle of the ocean and going down for the final count. But she also felt she had a lifeline. And it wasn't Carmine Serrano. She didn't know him from the man on the moon. It was James Serrano.

She turned her head toward him. "What can he do for her?" she asked.

"He can help us, Gina. He can help. Because you know what no bail means."

Gina nodded her head. "I know what it means. It means they intend to make Tamira an example."

"Right," said James. "They're going to give her prison time. As a juvenile, yes, but she'll still go to jail."

Gina's heart dropped.

"We know how it works, Gina," James said. "And I've been at this game a decade longer than you have. I know how it works more than you ever will. Our daughter is in trouble."

Gina leaned her head back again. "When that judge said no bail, my heart stopped. Evidence isn't going to matter. Truth isn't going to be pursued. They have every intention of making her the scapegoat and letting this Brandon Raglin and the rest of those kids off scot free."

"They haven't even arrested them," James said. "You notice that? They were in that car too when that girl was killed. But they haven't even arrested them."

Gina nodded. "Yes, I know that too."

They stopped at a red light, and James looked at her. "We need help, Genevieve."

Gina knew that too. "Whatever we have to do to get her out of that jail and those charges dropped," Gina said, "we have to do it."

James nodded. "Now you're talking my language," he said. And when that light turned green, he sped through the streets of Chicago, heading straight for his brother's house.

CHAPTER TWENTY-FOUR

Carmine Serrano was seated in a chair on his back patio skimming through a print edition of the Chicago Tribune that was spread out on the table. He wore shorts, an open shirt that revealed a slight belly on his stocky frame, and flipflops. His brother Vinny was seated at the table, too, trying to reason with him.

"All I want is a couple weeks' off, Carmine," he pleaded. "That's not too much to ask hard as I work for you. Just two weeks."

"And I told your ass it's bad timing," said Carmine, as he continued to turn a page.

"It's always bad timing with you. When's it ever good timing? I'll never go anywhere for as long as I live because there's never a good time to you. All I want is a little get away to rest my nerves and get my body back in shape, and you won't even let me do that!"

Vincent was a hysterical Italian, as Carmine put it, who always spoke as if he was acting in a stage play, with all the mannerisms and movements of a ham actor.

"You hearing me, Carmine?" Vincent

asked. "I need to get my body back in shape. I'm a wreck over here!"

Carmine looked at his kid brother. Vincent was in his early thirties and was in better shape than most twenty-year-olds. "Poor Vincent," Carmine said in that soft Italian-accented voice that dripped with sarcasm, the very opposite of his brother's voice. "I weep for poor Vincent. Rest your nerves, you say. Get your body back in shape, you say. What are you some fucking broad? Get the fuck out of here with that crap!"

"Carmine, please! Just a couple weeks. A little get away."

"Who with?" Carmine asked.

Vincent had not expected that question. "What?"

"What are you deaf? This get away. Who are you going with?"

"Oh!" Vincent hadn't thought that far ahead. "Nobody, Carmine. With myself."

"Bullshit! You wouldn't know what to do with yourself."

"Okay then." Carmine quickly regrouped. Am I gonna take a bird with me? Probably. But that's because I need help getting back up to par."

"Let Bruno go with you then. He'll get your ass back up to par."

Vincent frowned. "Gross!" he yelled, and Carmine laughed.

But then the alarm was sounded from the intercom on the table, and Carmine pressed button. "Who is it?" he asked.

"It's Jimmy, Boss. He just drove up with some dame."

"What dame?" Carmine asked.

"Some dame. Never seen her before."

"Maybe it's the bird he saved in that parking lot," Vincent said.

Carmine frowned, and released the intercom button. "What bird he saved? What parking lot?"

"I heard he was over at Donovan's office in Chicago when some car tried to run him over, but instead of trying to save himself, he seemed more concern with saving the bird that was with him."

Carmine was angry.

"What?" asked Vincent. "You didn't know?"

"It's the first I'm hearing about it," Carmine said. "And I don't like that."

"Damn!" Vincent said. "I thought you knew. I wouldn't have. . ."

Carmine looked at him. "You wouldn't have what? You wouldn't have said anything if you knew I didn't know? Go on and say it. I know you and Jimmy keeps secrets from me. But that's alright. All I do is give my life for your asses. That's alright."

Vincent could tell his brother was hurt. He and James were his world. He'd do anything for them, and they knew it. "I didn't mean anything by it, Carmine."

"You never do."

"I'm just saying maybe the dame that's with Jimmy is the same bird he saved in that parking lot. That's all I'm saying. I heard he was more concerned about her safety than he was about his own. That's why I thought it was strange."

"Strange is the word alright," said Carmine. "Our brother more concerned about some broad than he is about himself? I'll believe it when I see it."

"Just two weeks, Carmine," Vincent said, pleading his case again.

"I'm through with that," Carmine said bluntly.

"All I'm asking for is two little weeks," Vincent said just as James and Gina appeared on the far side of the huge patio and began slowly heading their way.

When Carmine didn't respond to him, Vincent looked at him. "Is it a no then?"

Carmine shook his head. "Are you brain

dead? It's a fucking no."

"But why?"

"I told your ass why!" Carmine said in such a strident voice that Gina stopped in her tracks when she heard it. She had zero experience with a mob boss, and her heart pounded. James placed his hand on her back. "It's okay," he said to her, and they began walking again.

But Carmine was still yelling at Vincent. "Until I figure out what's going on, and now with this new information you just told me, no vacations!"

Vincent was upset, but he knew arguing with his brother was the kind of dead-end street he didn't want to go down. He, instead, looked at James as he approached with the lady. "Nice looking dame," he said to Carmine. "I like that hair."

"Jimmy will snatch your eyeballs out you try to hit on that one," said Carmine, as he watched them too.

"Why would you say something like that? She's just another bird to Jimmy."

"If she's the bird he risked his life for, I don't think so. Besides," said Carmine, "she's got that look Jimmy likes."

Vincent grinned. "You mean because she's black?"

But James and Gina were upon them.

"Jimmy, my man," Vincent said. "What's shaking?"

"The 1980s?" James responded, and Carmine laughed.

"What are you doing here?" Vincent asked. "I don't normally see you here."

James looked at his younger brother. "Get lost. I need to have a conversation with Carmine."

"What a way to talk to somebody."

James gave him a harder look and Vincent got the message. "Alright already!" he said and rose to his feet. "Who's the bird?" he asked.

"Does she have wings, Vincent?"

Vincent was confused. Carmine wasn't. He was smiling. "Wings?" Vincent asked.

"Does it look like she can fly?"

Vincent frowned. "What are you getting at?" Then he realized what. "You use that term too. It's our culture, as if you don't remember. That's what we call dames in Carmine's world."

"Maybe you've been in Carmine's world too long," said James.

"And you haven't?" asked Vincent.

James paused. "I have too," he admitted.

Gina looked at James. She loved his honesty.

"So," asked Vincent with a beautiful smile, "who's the bird?"

James shook his head. His brother was hopeless. "This is Genevieve Griffin."

"Genna V what?" asked Vincent.

"Gina," said Gina as she extended her hand. "Nice to meet you."

"Nice to meet you," Vincent said, shaking her hand. "I'm Vinny. His brudder."

He said *brother* in such a funny way that Gina almost smiled. But she thought about why she was there at all, and she still couldn't muster a smile.

"Now get lost," said James.

"An asshole my brudder is," said Vincent. "Sure you wanna take that on?"

James gave Vincent another hard look. "I'm going!" Vincent said. But then he looked at Carmine one more time. "Just two weeks, Carmine," he pleaded.

"I'm through with that," Carmine said again.

"See how they do me?" Vincent said to Gina.

But then James thought about it. What he had to say was something Vincent needed to hear too. "You're right," he said to Vincent. "Stay."

Even Carmine looked at James. Vincent

was surprised. "You're sure?"

"Yes. Sit down, Vinny. You need to hear this too."

Vincent smiled. He was unaccustomed to being included when his big brothers had a serious powwow. He gladly sat down.

James and Gina sat down too.

Gina was staring at Carmine as she sat at the table. Almost everything about the man screamed mob boss to her. From the clothes he wore, to the way he talked and looked, she felt as if she was watching a mob movie just looking at him. The only thing that surprised her was how attractive he was. He wasn't gorgeous in the same way James and his brother Vinny were, but he had something more than that. He had a unique charm and charisma about him that seemed more dangerous, and he had the kind of animalistic sexuality that made her well aware that he was not the one to trifle with. Not just outside of the bedroom, either, but, she suspected, inside of it too.

In fact, everything about Carmine Serrano screamed pure power, and just being around him for those few minutes was already evoking a kind of terrifying fear within Gina. A part of her wanted to get up from that table and run. This man was the real deal, she thought. But another part of her knew she couldn't. They needed his help.

But did she really want to get in league with a man like him?

"What can I do you for?" Carmine asked his brother as he folded his newspaper, although he was looking at Gina. But he couldn't help it. She was a gorgeous girl to look at. "What brings you this way? Another parking lot incident?"

James frowned.

"Oh, yeah. I know about that. You didn't tell me shit about it though."

"Let me guess," said James. "Vinny told you?"

"How come he knew about that shit before I did, Jimmy?" Carmine asked, genuinely hurt.

"It was nothing."

"I give you permission to use my men any way you see fit," Carmine said. "You earned that right. But I don't like my men keeping secrets from me."

"It was nothing I couldn't handle, Carmine."

"You handled it?"

"Yeah."

Carmine stared at his brother. He wasn't sure if he believed him. "Why are you here?" he asked him.

James exhaled. "This is Gina Griffin," he said.

"I got that already. What you telling me that for? Nice to meet you, Gina," he said to Gina. "I'm Carmine, by the way. But since you're here, I'm sure you know that already. What's going on? Jimmy ain't never brought no dame around me."

Gina didn't think she had the nerve to say much of anything substantive to that man. He just seemed so hard. That was why she looked to James to explain the reason for their visit.

James looked at his brother. "Her daughter's in trouble," he said.

"Oh yeah? I'm sorry to hear that. How old is this daughter?"

"Fifteen," Gina said. She could manage that.

But Carmine was shaking his head. "Bad age," he said. "Shit goes down at that age. Real shit. What she do?"

"She didn't do anything," Gina said bluntly. And then she knew she had to clarify. "I mean, she did do something, but not what they're accusing her of."

"Okay, lady, back up," said Carmine. "You're telling a story like I already know this shit. What is she accused of?"

Gina's nerves around Carmine failed

again, and she looked to James again.

"She went joyriding with some friends," James said. "There was a bad accident. One of the girls in the car was killed."

"Damn," said Carmine in a way Gina could tell was heartfelt. He leaned back in his chair.

"She wasn't driving," James continued, "but the other kids claimed she was. She's been booked for vehicular homicide."

"How do you know she wasn't the driver?" Carmine asked.

"Because she said so," said Gina. "She said it emphatically."

"That's not what I'm talking about. Everybody in jail says they didn't do it. Nothing but innocent people in jail, let them tell it. I'm talking about what proof you have she wasn't the driver?"

"Proof?" Gina asked.

"Yeah, lady, proof," Carmine said in that soft-voiced-but-harsh tone of his. "I'm not talking what some teenager said. I'm talking proof. Do you got proof?"

Gina swallowed hard. "No," she said. "Not yet."

"Then what you want me to do? I'm just an honest joe trying to make an honest living out here."

"Her daughter, Carmine," said James, and then he frowned as if it pained him to have to admit it to two brothers who loved the meaning of family, but didn't have any of their own outside of their brotherhood.

And then James blurted it out. "Her daughter is my daughter too," he said.

At first, Carmine frowned. And then he stared at his brother. Vincent did too. "Say what now?" Vincent asked him, shocked beyond measure.

James still found it hard to believe himself. "Her daughter, whose name is Tamira, is my daughter too."

"You got a daughter?" Vincent asked as if he had been sleeping his life away and missed something that monumental. "And she's *fifteen*?!"

James nodded. "Yes."

"How could you keep a secret like that from your own family?" Vincent asked him.

"He didn't know," Gina quickly defended him. "He just found out."

"After she got in trouble?" Vincent asked, as if it was some kind of trap. "How convenient."

James looked at his younger brother. "No, Vinny," he said. "We just hooked back up again."

"After fifteen years?" asked Carmine.

"Yes."

Carmine seemed floored to Gina. And doubtful too. She wondered if he was going to be okay. He even leaned forward and looked at James. "You're sure about this, Jimmy?"

"I'm positive, Carmine."

"How can you be so positive so fast? No disrespect to the lady here, but you got DNA to prove this?"

"No. No need."

Carmine frowned. "Whatta you mean no need? Get the fuck out of here with that no need bullshit. I know you wanna trust her and you believe every word she say---"

"It's not a matter of trust," said James.

"Then what is it a matter of, Mister Educated?"

"The girl, my daughter, looks exactly like Vincent looked when he was her age."

Vincent smiled. "Really? So she's supposedly great looking then?"

"She's my daughter, Carmine," James made clear, ignoring Vincent. "I knew it as soon as I saw her."

"But we'll get a DNA test," said Gina. "I have no problem with that at all."

Carmine nodded. "Good," he said. "Because looks can be deceiving," he added, looking at Gina.

Gina felt horrible, as if he viewed her as some gold digger trying to trap James or something, but she would be suspicious if she were in his shoes too. Besides, it wasn't about her nor James. It was about Tamira. "Can you help us?" she asked him.

Carmine leaned back. He looked from Gina to James and then to Vincent, as if he was trying to picture the girl in his own head. And it felt like he could go either way to Gina. As if he could help them, or tell them to get lost.

He decided to help. For James's sake, he picked up his cell phone, thumbed through it, found the private number he was looking for, and then made the call.

When a woman answered the phone, he spoke up. "I need to speak to the Mayor," he said into his phone.

Gina glanced at James. The mayor? Was he for real?

"May I ask who's calling?" the lady on the phone said.

"It's Carmine Serrano."

"One moment please, Mr. Serrano. I'll see if he's available."

"He'd better be available," Carmine said in a lower tone, but Gina heard him.

Then the mayor came onto the line. "Carmine, how are you?"

"I'm good. You?"

"Couldn't be better!"

"That's good to hear."

"How's your golf game? Improved?"

"Golf game. What golf game?"

The mayor laughed. "I'm in a slump myself," he said. "I can't see the green. I can't see the hole. I can't see shit out there anymore."

"Yeah, we all have slumps like that," Carmine said. "My swing ain't what it used to be either. But listen, I don't wanna take up too much of your time. I know you're a busy man. But I need a favor."

As Carmine made spoke with the mayor, James reached out and placed Gina's hand in his hand. They were finally getting to the end of that tunnel they were in, he felt.

Gina felt it too. But she wasn't seeing light at the end of the tunnel yet, as James were. She was still stuck on the fact that James's brother could just pick up the phone and call the Mayor of Chicago! Did that mean the mayor was corrupt too? Did that mean the mayor, a man she voted for, has mob ties too?

And when Carmine ended the call, she still wasn't sure if there finally was any light. "It'll be tonight," he said. "They'll call you with the details."

"Thanks, Carmine," James said.

Gina didn't know what they were thanking him for, but she thanked him too. And then James and Gina stood up.

"And Jimmy?" Carmine said.

They both looked at him.

"When you get that call, take fifty grand with you."

Gina's heart dropped. Fifty thousand dollars? Were they paying somebody off? How would James get his hands on that kind of money so fast?

But then she realized who she was dealing with. It was only then did it sink in that she was crossing a line and it could all blow up in their faces. She had to hope Carmine Serrano knew what he was doing. She knew James did.

And when James nodded his assent, she trusted him and left that alone. Then James took Gina's hand, and they made their way out of Carmine's world.

But Vincent was still giddy. He was still smiling. "She looks like me, Carmine," he said. "Can you imagine that? Some kid looks like me? What you got to say about that?"

Carmine was still worried about James. "Heaven help her," he said to his baby brother, without cracking a smile.

CHAPTER TWENTY-FIVE

At James's house, they were hugged up on his sofa, both with a glass of wine in their hands. It was already after eight. They were waiting for the call. And both of them had Tamira on their minds.

James kissed Gina's forehead. "What are we going to tell her?" he asked.

"Depends," said Gina.

"On what?"

"On whether or not you plan to stick around. Not for me," Gina quickly pointed out. "But for Tamira."

James had her fingers interlaced with his and he kept moving their fingers around. "I plan to stick around," he said, "for both of you. I want to get to know both of you better. Then I'm hoping we can find a way to pull it all together. To be a family." Then he smiled. "Fifteen years late."

"I don't want her hurt," Gina said, still focused exclusively on Tamira. "I don't want you to leave her even if me and you don't work out. That's what I mean."

"I won't leave," James said, but Gina

leaned up and looked over at him, as if she had to see him say it to believe him.

"I won't leave her, Gina. I promise you that," he said firmly.

Gina, satisfied, leaned back against him, and began playing with their fingers too. "Then we'll tell her after those charges have been dropped, and she's free again."

"Yes. That sounds sensible. But you always are, aren't you?"

"I always am what?"

"Sensible."

Gina smiled. "Hardly," she said.

"It must have been difficult."

Gina waited. "What must have been difficult?"

"Raising her alone."

Gina nodded. "Very difficult. Girls are never easy to raise, and Tamira is no pushover. She's very feisty and independent and tough."

"Sounds like good qualities to me."

Gina smiled. "I agree!"

"You know what?"

Gina looked over at him. "What?"

James looked at her. "I'm going to enjoy being with you." He almost said *for the rest of my life*, but he didn't want to scare her. They had a lot of getting to know each other to do before he would make that pronouncement, even though that was exactly how he felt. "And I'm not just talking about sexually either, although I am talking about that too."

Gina smiled. "You would," she said, and he laughed.

And then he laid down on the sofa, and he pulled her on top of him. She laid her head on his chest, he wrapped his arms around her, and then they closed their eyes. Just to try to regain some strength for the long haul they knew was in front of them. They fell asleep almost immediately.

Three hours later, as if a testament to their raw nerves, as soon as they heard James's cell phone ringing, they both woke up as if they'd been startled.

James removed one of his arms from around Gina and grabbed his phone from off of the coffee table. "This is Jim," he said anxiously.

Then he listened. And listened some more. And then he ended the call.

"Who was it?" Gina asked.

James moved her off of him and then stood up. "The meeting's set," he said.

Gina stood up. "Where?"

"On Mulligan in an hour. Under the streetlight. But I'm getting over there right now."

He picked up the briefcase filled with the cash he was told to take with him.

Gina stood to her feet. "Why can't I go with you?" she asked him.

"Because I don't want any blowback on you if anything goes south," James made clear. "This isn't Tiddlywinks. This is hardcore underground. You will know nothing about this. For your own sake. For our daughter's sake. Tamira will need you. That's why," he said and began heading for the door.

Gina followed him. And she wasn't going to fight it because she knew he spoke the truth. She had to stay back for Tamira's sake. But when they got to the door, she pulled him into her arms. "Please be careful, James," she said.

He looked down at her. His feelings for her seemed to be intensifying with every passing moment he spent with her. He kissed her on her lips. "I'll be safe," he said. "Don't worry about me. I'll be just fine."

"Call me when you're on your way back."

"I will." Then he smiled.

"What?"

"I don't have your cell phone number."

Gina smiled. "I don't have yours either," she said, and they exchanged cell phones and exchanged numbers.

And then James kissed her again, and left.

When he walked out, she closed the door

behind him and locked it. And suddenly she felt alone again. Just like that. She felt alone.

She leaned against the door and rubbed her forehead. She could only imagine what little hope she would have had if this would have happened and James was not in her life. The Judge and DA were already telegraphing their plans to scapegoat Tamira. They were already more than willing to lock up an innocent girl in the name of protecting those who looked more like them. Gina saw it all the time whenever she had cases in that same courthouse. But only this time it was her daughter they were trying to game.

She closed her eyes. And just stood there. And then her phone began ringing.

When she looked at the Caller ID, she answered it. And made her way back toward the sofa. "Hey, Kim."

"How are you, girl?"

"I'm here." She sat down on the sofa with one leg beneath her butt.

"How did it go?"

Gina had forgotten all about telling Kim. She exhaled. "They denied bail," she said.

"Really? Why?"

"They want to railroad her. Why else?"

"Dang. What are you going to do?"

Gina would have told Kim about the plan,

but she wasn't going that far. Kim was great, but she could talk too much sometimes. "James is working on it," was all she was willing to say.

But that apparently said it all to Kim. "She'll get off then, if he's on the case," she said.

"Why would you say that?"

"I saw him, remember? I saw how he insisted on driving you to the hospital. He likes you. No doubt about it. He'll do whatever he can for you."

Gina felt like they were clicking, too, but she couldn't think about that right now. Tamira's freedom was all she could think about now. "Anyway," she said, "let me get off of this phone in case James tries to call me."

"He can still call you with me on the phone, GG. But I get your point. You want to be sure. Call me, though, if you hear something."

"I will, Kim. And thanks for caring."

They said their goodbyes, and ended the call.

But just as Gina was leaning back on the sofa, and decided to thumb through her camera gallery at pictures of Tamira, she heard what she thought was a sound in the kitchen. She was certain nobody was supposed to be in that big house, but she wondered if a servant might have been there too? There was no way James could keep that big a house clean all by himself.

She got up and made her way through the living room, then the dining room, and then into the kitchen. It was dark in the kitchen and she turned on the light. And a man was standing there!

First, she screamed, startled out of her skin. But could he be a servant? "Who are you?" she asked him.

But when she realized he had a butcher's knife in his hand, and a menacing look on his face, and he was slowly walking toward her, she didn't wait around for his answer. She ran. She ran and screamed and screamed and ran.

The man took off after her, running too, as they both made their way to that front door.

Gina had never been more afraid in her life. She knew she had to get out of that door to stand any chance of survival. That was why she ran faster than she'd ever run before. And she made it to the door.

But just as she unlocked it and had flung it open, that intruder grabbed her from behind, slinging her by her hair, and then he flung her away from that door and slammed it back shut.

Down on the floor with a hard drop, Gina backed up on her butt, and then scrambled to her feet. As the intruder progressed toward her, she started throwing everything she could get her hands on at him, including lamps and vases and anything else she touched. But he had that knife, and he was upon her, and he grabbed her up and slammed her against the wall as if she were a feather. And then he pinned her there. With that knife, that huge, sharp knife, at her throat.

CHAPTER TWENTY-SIX

James answered his ringing phone just as he turned a corner. His car screen noted that it was Josh Bronson, one of Carmine's security chiefs, so he answered quickly. "What you got for me, Bronze?"

"We reviewed every camera in that area, Boss. Every single one. But we couldn't find that car in any frame. It was as if whoever was driving that car knew exactly what they were doing. They avoided every camera. They went down every side street and back street they could find."

"Until the wreck," James said.

"Until the wreck. And that wasn't on camera either. They knew what they were doing."

"So we got nothing, in other words," James said.

"That's the size of it, yeah."

"Okay, Bronze, thanks."

"And I still have a crew working on the Joey Raglin matter. But they haven't turned up anything on that case yet either."

James frowned. "Joey Raglin?"

"Yeah, Boss. Porterhouse Joe? That's

his name. Billy Brown in the safe house claimed Porter was the one who paid him to try to take you out in that parking lot. Remember?"

James, stunned, suddenly slammed on brakes, and pulled over to the side of the road. "Are you telling me that Porterhouse Joe's real name is Raglin?"

"Yeah. Why?"

And suddenly Gina's face flashed before James's eyes and he felt a sense of dread he couldn't explain. He immediately ended the call with Bronson and phoned Gina. But he didn't get an answer.

But that dread didn't ease. It intensified. And it was palpable. He slung a U-turn in the middle of the road, and took off. He flew.

But back at his house, Gina felt as if time was standing still. Because her tormentor was tormenting her. He still had her pinned against that wall. He still was teasing her neck with that very sharp knife. He still was looking his ugly, beady eyes at her smooth skin. And he started licking her.

Gina felt her skin crawl as he licked her, and she wanted to kick him in the groin, or do something even worse than that, but that knife was too close to her neck. Any false move and she could be slashed and bleed-out for sure.

That was why she remained still as she could. That was why, other than shaking like a leaf, she dared not to even cry as he licked her.

But then he seemed to have had enough of the easy stuff. He seemed to want more. He grabbed Gina by the neck, with that knife still pressed against her, and dragged her onto the sofa. He threw her on the sofa and got on top of her. He sat the knife on the side table.

When he did that, Gina started fighting again. He had her hands and arms pinned, but she was kicking her feet with all she had to try and bend her legs to kick him. But his big body was on top of her small body, and she was just kicking at air.

But then he lost his grip on one of her hands and she took her fingers and tried to gouge his eyes out.

"Bitch!" he yelled as the pain ripped through is body and he punched her hard across her face.

Gina was in pain too, from his punch, but she kept resisting him, trying to use all she had to break free from him. But his size and strength overwhelmed her easily and he angrily placed her hands over her head, and held them both in his grasp with one of his hands. Then he pulled out zip ties with his other hand and began frantically tying her hands together.

When he had tied her up so that her hands were no longer useful to her, he smiled, and grabbed his knife. He placed it against her face this time. "I like'em feisty," he said. And then his look turned lustful and he began unbuttoning her blouse with one hand while he continued to tease her with that knife in his other hand.

"She told me all about you and him," the man said as he slowly unbuttoned her. "And about the girl. It was more than we could have ever hoped for."

"Who are you?" Gina asked. She knew if she kept him talking, it might prolong the inevitable.

"I was following Serrano. That was my job. To follow him without him ever knowing he was being followed. And he went to your office. That law office. So I went in, too, and pretended to be a new client. And while he was in that office talking to you about whatever he was talking to you about, that secretary of yours, that Kim, was giving me the tea. All the tea. Couldn't keep her mouth shut she was so excited you wrangled yourself a rich man. I pretended I couldn't afford you because no way I had the kind of money whoever drove that Maybach drove that was parked in front of your office. I knew it was Serrano's car, but that's how I said it. Kim said the guy it belonged to wasn't even a client. That you and the guy had a history together, that was why she think he was there. And then she ultimately told me that she thinks the two of you had a kid together back in the day."

He smiled when her naked breasts appeared. "I'm going to enjoy this," he said.

"What about the kid?" Gina asked nervously.

"This part ain't in the plan," the intruder said, still staring at her breasts, "but the fact that you're hot as hell wasn't in the plan either. I'm putting it in the plan."

Gina swallowed hard. She had to keep him talking! "What did you do when Kim told you we had a child together?" she asked him.

He got distracted again. "That was all I needed to hear," he said. "A kid together? I knew Boss would love that news. So, I pretended to go next door to get a coffee, but I really went and called the boss. To see what he wanted me to do about this news. And as soon as I told him, he said to forget about Serrano and go after the girl."

Gina's heart dropped.

The intruder continued. "He said that would be poetic justice. Go after the girl. And we came up with a plan."

But his eyes were becoming too lust-filled to finish any story, and he slowly began to move his mouth toward Gina's breasts.

But before he could touch them, he felt two big, hard hands on his body and then his body was jerked backwards with a jerk that took his breath away.

"He's got a knife!" Gina yelled to James, who had entered the house from the same back door the intruder had entered, and he immediately grabbed the intruder's hand that contained the knife and ran with him across the room until his back hit the wall. He had to keep the man alive to get some answers. And he had to dislodge that knife.

But that hard slam against the wall didn't help. It didn't dislodge the knife.

The two men began struggling for control of that knife in an epic battle of strength against strength.

But Gina was there too. And she didn't remain on that sofa like some fragile flower. He almost raped her. She was as angry as James.

She jumped up quickly and ran to the two men. She knew she couldn't match either one of them in strength, but she had her wits about her.

She began feeling James's pockets as he and the intruder were trying to overwhelm each other so desperately that veins were appearing on their foreheads. And then she felt what she was searching for. It was in his opposite pocket. And she pulled it out quickly and immediately aimed it at the side of the intruder's face so that he could see what she had.

"Drop that knife," she yelled, "or with every ounce of strength I have I'll blow your brains out!"

The intruder was no fool. He was staring down the barrel of a gun at a knife fight. He released his grip on the knife, and James easily took it from him.

Then James tossed that knife aside, took his gun from Gina, and began to pistol whip the intruder who almost raped his woman with a madman's vengeance.

James hit that intruder and he hit him. He had the intruder bent sideways in agony as he hit him until he saw blood. Until the white meat.

Gina had never seen a man beat another man so viciously. But she'd already seen that James had it in him. She'd already determined that.

But James wasn't a man out of control. He was a man trying to exert control. He couldn't let that asshole get away with harming Gina, and he had to make that clear.

But he had his wits about him too. He managed to stop himself. Because they needed answers, not a dead body.

Breathing heavily, he grabbed the intruder and then dragged him to the sofa, where he dropped him there.

The intruder was bleeding profusely, and his blood was all over the place, but neither James nor Gina concerned themselves with his medical issue. They needed answers.

"He kept talking about a boss, James," Gina quickly alerted him as they stood in front of the intruder that was now their prisoner. "He said Kim mentioned to him that we had a child together, and his boss paid him to take Tam out."

James was shocked. "Who's your boss?" James asked him. "And don't fuck me around or I'll finish the job, motherfucker. Who's the boss?"

And the intruder, knowing his body wasn't going to take any more beat downs, didn't beat around. He answered his question. "Raglin," he said.

Gina frowned. And then she was shocked. "Raglin? Isn't that the last name of the driver of the car, James?"

"Yes," said James. But he was still staring at their intruder. "So Porterhouse sent you?"

The intruder frowned. "Who?"

James was about to grab him again. "Didn't I tell you not to fuck with me!"

"I'm not!" the intruder yelled. "I've never heard of no Porterhouse!"

James stopped grabbing the intruder and looked at him. "You said Raglin."

"That's who sent me. Not no Porterhouse."

By now, James was baffled. He released his grasp on the intruder and stood erect again. "Raglin who?" he asked him.

"Merv Raglin," the intruder said.

James frowned. "Who?"

"Merv Raglin! The man I work for. He sent me."

James had never heard of any Merv Raglin. "Where is he?" he asked him.

"Here. In Chicago. He don't live here though, so I don't know where he's staying." His blood loss was making him weak. "I need a doctor, man," he said.

"Where's he from?" James asked him.

"Latham," the intruder said.

When James and Gina heard the name of the town, they both froze. It was the town where they met, and ended up having Tamira.

James frowned. "What does he do in

Latham?" he asked him.

"I don't know! He hired me to do what I was doing. To follow you. He said some other guy was supposed to take you out, but he failed. He wanted me to follow you until he gave the order to take you out. But when I told him about your kid, he changed the plan."

James frowned. "How would he know . . ." Then he remembered what Gina had said about Kim.

"He pretended to be a client and Kim told him she thought Tamira was your child. She didn't mean anything by it, James. She just talk too damn much sometimes. I'll handle her."

"You'd better," James said. But it still wasn't adding up. How would this Raglin know anything about Tamira? "How did he find out who our daughter was?"

"He pulled background on her," the intruder said, motioning at Gina. "He found out who her daughter was, and where she attended school. Then he took it from there. "I need help," the intruder said, but he really was biding his time. "I'll bleed out. I need help, man."

But James and Gina weren't giving him a second glance. And the intruder saw it too. And he made his move.

While they still seemed to be trying to wrap their brains around the fact that Tamira got roped into it, and that there was no accident what happened to her, the intruder jumped up suddenly and deftly attempted to take the gun out of James's hand.

But James was adept, too, and his lax grip tightened just as the intruder attempted to snatch it. And the two men were in a struggle again.

Gina hurried to retrieve the knife that had been slung across the room as the two men struggled. But by the time she grabbed that knife, the gun was moving toward the chest area. And by the time she attempted to run behind the intruder to place that knife at his back and scare him into surrendering again, the gun went off.

Gina screamed out and backed away in total horror when she didn't know which one had been shot. They both were staring into each other's eyes as if they were in a state of suspended disbelief.

And then the intruder slowly slid down James's body, and dropped dead to the floor.

And Gina exhaled. Other than getting that call from the hospital, she had never been more afraid in her life. And she dropped that knife and fell into his arms. "I thought it was you," she cried. "I thought it was you!"

But James held her tightly. Because for

a second he thought it was him too. Then he pulled out his phone and ordered Bronson to get a clean-up crew to his house.

They both looked around at the mess their intruder had created. "There's blood everywhere," Gina said.

"It's not as if it didn't need renovating anyway," James said, and she looked at him. "It's about time I put the stamp of approval of a different woman on this house."

Gina was so relieved that James was okay that she managed to smile.

He loved her strength, and the fact that she was able to smile in the midst of such horror. And he was about to pull her into his arms again.

But then her eyes opened wider. "James!" she cried.

James's heart began to pound again. "What?" he asked her. "What's wrong?"

"You were supposed to meet that man on Mulligan Street. To help Tamira."

James had forgotten! He quickly looked at his Rolex. "I still have time," he said.

"I can't stay here," Gina said. "Not with that body."

"I know," James said, grabbing her by the hand. "Carmine's men will take care of this."

"Are you sure it's not your men too?" Gina asked him. It was the second time she had broached the subject about his possible involvement in his brother's obvious crime syndicate.

But this time there was no denial. He stopped and placed both hands on her arms. "Just know," he said, "that all this shit we have to do won't come back on you. We know what we're doing. Okay?"

Gina nodded. "Okay," she said.

"Now let's go," he said, and grabbed her hand.

Gina took note of that non-denial as she allowed him, who was moving even faster than she was, to pull her along. They hurried out the door.

CHAPTER TWENTY-SEVEN

The car was already parked in the business district on Mulligan Street, under the streetlamp as promised, and James parked his Mercedes-Maybach beside the car. But when the driver of the car got out, Gina, who sat on the front passenger seat beside James, froze. Not only was she shocked that it was a woman, but that it was the woman from court. The DA on Tamira's case! The one who didn't want to give her bail. She looked at James.

"Everybody's got a price, Genevieve," he said. "Never forget that."

But when Donna Finch got into James's car and sat on the backseat, she was as shocked as Gina was. "Whoa," she said when she realized they weren't alone. "Who's that?"

"That's Tamira's mother," James said. "She was at counsel table with me today."

But Finch was getting back out of the car. "I can't do it like this," she said.

"Wait a minute," James said anxiously, and he and Gina quickly turned around. "Just wait a minute!"

"I was asked to do this favor for

Carmine," Finch said with hysteria in her voice. "I was told nobody would be at this meeting, or know about this meeting, except for you and Carmine. Then you show up with another attorney? Are you kidding me?"

"She's the mother of the defendant."

"I don't give a shit who she is!" Finch yelled. "I can't do this and let her hold it over my head later, when her daughter's free and clear. Not happening," she said, and got out of the car.

"But what about my daughter?" Gina asked anxiously as she jumped out of the car too. James quickly got out on the driver's side as well. "What can we do about my daughter?" Gina was in a state of near-panic. She couldn't let that lady just leave!

Finch paused, and then exhaled. "Get me something on Brandon Raglin," she said, "and I'll drop the charges. But I have to have irrefutable proof that can hold up against all those students and their parents who are more than willing to point their fingers at your daughter. Irrefutable proof," she added, and then got into her car, and took off.

Gina looked at James. "What was she going to do for us for all of that money?"

"Manufacture evidence against Raglin," said James. "Because she knows, like we know, that Tamira's telling the truth and no way would a nineteen-year-old boy be in his own car with fifteen-year-olds, and not be behind the wheel."

"What do we do now?" Gina asked, her face a mask of worry.

"You heard her. We find dirt. Something I happen to be good at. Get back in the car," he ordered, and they did. And then he sped away.

CHAPTER TWENTY-EIGHT

Brandon Raglin was on the treadmill and he was running more than he was walking. A specimen of a young man, Brandon was running so fast that James, across the room in sweats, could hardly keep up. But that wasn't why he was there anyway. He was in the back of the gym, well out of eyeshot of the young man, running on a treadmill too. But as soon as Brandon finished, and made his way to the lockers, James casually discontinued his own treadmill runs and made his way back there too.

By the time James made his way in the back, Brandon had grabbed his towel and was headed for the showers. And just as Brandon had removed his gym shorts and entered the shower stall, James walked in and looked around. Confident nobody else was back there, he then hurried up to the young man.

Brandon was clueless as he moved to turn on the water tap. But before he could reach it, he suddenly felt a thick arm come around his neck, putting him in the grips of a chokehold, and a big hand covered his mouth, muffling the scream he tried to scream. And then he felt the big body that was behind him thrust him further into the stall and slam him against the wall.

"You know who I am?" James asked him breathlessly, both men sweaty from their workout. Only James was fully cloth in a pair of sweatpants and a jersey. "Do you know who I am?" James asked again, tightening the chokehold on Brandon's neck.

"No," Brandon said.

"Try again."

Brandon had his hands still on James's arm, trying to loosen his hold.

"Try again!" James said with clenched teeth.

"You're that girl's father," said Brandon. "You're Tamira's father."

It was the first time somebody had referred to James that way, and it made him all the more determined to take down every one of those fuckers who were trying to take Tamira down. "You were the driver. Weren't you?"

Tears were in Brandon's eyes. But when James tightened his grip even more, he nodded. "Yes," he said quickly, still trying to loosen that chokehold; barely able to breath.

"Why did you put the blame on my daughter?"

"I was ordered to! I got a couple guys from her school and gave them a thousand bucks each to help me pick up Tamira and couple of her girlfriends before school, and then we'd go have some fun."

"And that accident?"

"Staged," Brandon admitted. "I can hardly breath, Mister!"

"How was it staged?"

"I texted him what side she was sitting on, and he was supposed to hit the car on that side and kill her, without harming anybody else. But when he hit, the car flung around unexpectedly and he hit it again on the wrong side. The side where that other girl was sitting."

"Who was driving that SUV?" James asked. It had taken off after the crash, and the cops were supposedly looking for the driver. "Who was driving that SUV?"

"My old man," Brandon said.

"Who's your old man?"

"Merv Raglin."

At least the kid was giving him the name he expected to hear, James thought. "Any kin to the man we call Porterhouse Joe? Joey Raglin?"

"Yeah," Brandon said, still struggling to loosen James's grip. "He's my uncle."

James at least had a connection now. It

was no sick coincidence. "Where can I find this uncle of yours?"

"I don't know. Me and my old man are in town waiting for him to tell us what to do next. We got that girl in jail, and we paid all the other kids to point a finger at her as the driver, but we don't know what else he wants."

"How do you get in touch with him?"

"We don't! He gets in touch with us."

"From where?"

"I don't know."

"What about your old man? Would he know?"

Brandon's breath was becoming irregular again. James loosened his grip again. "Answer my question, motherfucker. Does your old man know where I can find Porterhouse?"

"I don't know."

"Where is his ass? And don't tell me you don't know that either."

"Outside," Brandon said.

James was floored. Did he hear him right? "What do you mean?"

"He was in the gym earlier, trying to get a workout in too. But he didn't last but ten minutes. He's outside in the car waiting for me."

James was anxious now. He would finally get some much-needed answers. "Let's go," he said.

"But I need to take a shower," said Brandon.

James angrily tightened his grip on Brandon. "You think I'm fucking with you, you rat bastard?" Then he pulled the gun he had in his sweatpants pocket and pressed it against Brandon's temple. "Try stupid shit with me and your stupid ass is dead. You and your old man. Do we understand each other?"

Brandon nodded nervously.

"Now let's go!" James ordered, and all but threw Brandon out of that shower stall. Brandon put back on his clothes quickly, and they left.

CHAPTER TWENTY-NINE

Outside, James had a baseball cap pushed down over his forehead as he walked slightly away from Brandon. James's goal was to stay at an angle that the man in the car across the parking lot, presumably Merv Raglin, would not be able to see James's approach too. It was the early morning hours in the nearly deserted parking lot, and a man walking with his son would have been suspicious.

And for the most part James's angle-walking seemed to work. Merv was still reading the print version of a newspaper he had in his hands and seemed none the wiser. It was working. Until they were within striking distance of the car and Brandon suddenly decided to go rogue.

Brandon apparently made the calculation that James needed them alive, not dead, and therefore he could take a chance. And he did. He took off running toward the car and screaming at his father. "Get out of here!" he started yelling at his father. "We've got to get out of here!"

James, realizing what the kid was doing, took off running toward Brandon and that car too.

Merv Raglin heard his son's scream and turned in his direction. When he saw him running as if he was running for his life, and then saw the man he recognized as Jimmy Serrano running after him, he quickly pressed the Start button on his Ford. When his son jumped into the backseat of the car on the driver's side, he took off.

But not before James reached out and grabbed the back door that Brandon had opened, and held onto that still-open door as Merv Raglin took off.

At first Merv tried to go into circles, to force James's grip to loosen, but James had a death grip on that door and was hanging on for dear life. He was flying around with every circle Merv was making with that car, but he was hanging on. Because James had a calculation too. He calculated that he wasn't about to let those fuckers get away.

And even when Merv Raglin suddenly slammed on brakes, James nearly fell off, but he still held on. And Merv, realizing it too, quickly continued driving. But instead of continuing to drive in circles, Merv decided to take off out of the parking lot where he could drive faster.

James knew he would be a dead man if Merv was able to get out of that parking lot and go full speed on the road, but he continued to hold on. Until he suddenly saw, from across the parking lot, his Mercedes-Maybach speeding toward that exit too. And James's heart fell through his shoe. Because Gina, who had been ordered by him to wait in the car, was driving his car. And she was determined to stop Merv too. She was determined to make sure whomever was driving that car didn't hit the road with James still holding on.

And she did it. She sped in front of that Ford and slammed on brakes, causing that Ford to swerve violently. James jumped from the car as it tilted on two wheels and then began to roll over repeatedly, as if it were a toy. Until it stopped rolling and rested upright.

But James was more worried about Gina than he was about the Raglins. He hurried to his car just as Gina was getting out. But she was fine. And his car, which had avoided a collision altogether, was fine too.

But then Gina pointed toward the wrecked Ford. "He's trying to get away, James!" she yelled, and James looked too.

Old Man Raglin had dragged his injured

body out of the Ford and was making a run for it. But one of his legs had been badly injured in the rollover and he had to drag it along. It was obvious he wasn't going to get very far.

"Wait in the car," he ordered Gina, as he ran toward the totaled Ford. Figuring Brandon would be a bigger threat at that point than the old man, he looked into the wrecked car before he went to pursue Merv. But Brandon was upside down in the car, his eyes wide open. He was already dead. There was no doubt about it. He wore no seat belt, which meant that rollover caused him to fly around in that vehicle like a human projectile, and it crushed him.

But James could feel no sympathy for somebody willing to destroy a young girl's life for whatever monetary reward they might get in the end. He took off after Merv Raglin. And when he easily caught up with Merv and knocked him to the ground, he placed him in a chokehold, too. He was pleased to see Gina, in his Mercedes, speeding up to where they were. Because he was, by this point, completely exhausted.

Gina slammed on brakes when she made it up to James. "Get in before the cops come," she yelled at James as if she were Bonnie and he was Clyde. But he knew where her anxiety was coming from. She had to have figured the man in James's clutches had information that could potentially free her child. She was willing to pull out all the stops to make that happen, even if it meant skirting the law she cherished since that law wasn't cherishing her daughter's freedom. James grabbed Merv, threw him in the backseat, and got in with him. Once he closed the door, Gina took off.

Merv started crying, grieving for his son, but James had no sympathy. A girl was dead and his daughter was in jeopardy of going to prison for many years. He grabbed Merv by his collar. "Who's bankrolling you and your son?"

"Brandon's dead," Merv said, his voice cracking with emotion. Gina looked through the rearview as she drove. She hated to hear it, but it wasn't as if they didn't bring it on themselves.

James felt the same way as he tightened his grip on Merv's collar. "Who's behind all of this? I'm not asking again!"

"Porter," Merv finally said.

"Who's Porter?" James asked, although he already knew.

"Joey Raglin. Porterhouse Joe. My brother."

James exhaled. Finally the closest link. "What's his beef with me and my daughter?" James asked.

"His daughter," said Merv.

"What? What about his daughter?" James asked.

Merv started crying hysterically. "Brandon's gone!"

"What about his daughter?" James asked just as angrily.

But Merv wasn't listening anymore. His grief was overwhelming. So overwhelming that he suddenly flung open the door of James's car and attempted to throw himself out of the speeding car.

James tried to hold onto him with all he had, and Gina slammed on brakes, but Merv was more determined than both of them. Merv fell out of the car.

They both looked behind them as Merv's body rolled and rolled until it wrapped itself around a tree.

Gina pulled to the side of the road and James jumped out and ran to the body.

Remarkably, he thought, Merv was still alive. But just barely. James got on his knees so that his mouth could be at Merv's ear. He had to have answers!

"What about Porter's daughter?" James asked frantically. "What about his daughter?"

But Merv was still grieving his son. "Brandon. Brandon!"

James was getting nowhere fast, and

Merv was not going to last very much longer. "Where's Porterhouse?" James asked anxiously. When that went nowhere, James angrily turned Merv's face to his face, to get him to focus. "Where's Porter?" he asked.

It was only then did Merv respond. "Paying a visit," he said.

"A visit to whom?" James asked.

"He ordered the hit."

James frowned. "Who ordered what hit?"

"Carmine Serrano. He ordered the hit. Porter's taking care of him right now!"

James's heart dropped. And he quickly got up and started running to his car, pulling out his cell phone.

"Get to Carmine's house!" he yelled at Gina as he jumped into his car. "Get to Carmine's house!"

And Gina didn't hesitate. She took off just as James was calling Carmine. Just as Merv Raglin was taking his last and final breath.

CHAPTER THIRTY

As Gina sped through the streets of Chicago heading to Carmine's house, James had been unsuccessful in reaching, not only Carmine, but any of his security apparatus on site. Then he called Bronson to get backup to Carmine's, and then he called Vinny to get to Carmine's too. He didn't know who was closer, but he knew his brother was in trouble or somebody at his estate would have answered by now.

And James's suspicion was realized when they arrived at Carmine's estate. None of the armed men usually at his security gate were present. And when James pressed a button in his car that was able to override the code at his brother's house and the gate opened and they entered the grounds, they saw the carnage.

The bodies of Carmine's security detail were piled up, as if they were being hid from public view on the inside of the gate. And James recognized them all. Some worked the gate. Some worked the grounds. But they all were dead.

And Gina was thrown. She'd kept it together up until she saw all those bodies! She froze. She couldn't drive another inch.

James saw it too, but he knew he couldn't leave her out in that car alone. "I know this is difficult, sweetie," he said to her. But Gina still looked bewildered. "Look at me, Genevieve."

Gina looked at him.

"I know it's hard," James said to her frightened face, "but I can't leave you in this car alone. I don't know how many are inside, or still outside. I don't know what's going on. But the answers we need are inside. You've got to come with me, okay?"

Gina nodded. "Okay."

"I'll protect you. Okay?"

Gina nodded again. She believed him. "Okay."

And then they got out of the car, James took Gina's hand, and they ran around the back of the house.

To their surprise, Vincent was already there and was just about to go inside.

"Where did you park?" James asked him as they met up at the backdoor.

"On the back street," said Vincent. "Then I came on foot. I saw the bodies around front." Then he looked beyond his brother. "You think it's a good idea having her here?"

"No choice," said James, and then he went up to the door, checked that the door was locked, and then he punched the combination on the lock to get inside.

Once inside, they heard nothing and saw no one. Which only made the situation more tense. Was an ambush waiting for them? How many men did Porterhouse have with him?

Then, suddenly, gunfire erupted upstairs and Vincent began to run through the kitchen toward the living room. But James stopped him. "The back way!" he whispered. And all three ran up the backstairs.

When they made it on the second-floor landing, they saw Porterhouse Joe running out of Carmine's bedroom and Carmine, with a gun in hand, was chasing after him.

"Carmine!" James yelled to him from the other end of the hall. "How many?"

"Just this asshole!" Carmine said, and was about to fire on him.

"No!" James yelled. "We need him!"

"Then you'd better not let his ass get away!" Carmine ordered, and James and Vincent ran toward him.

"Keep her," James said to his brother, handing off Gina to him, as he and Vincent ran down the stairs.

Carmine grabbed Gina's hand. "What a place for a dame right now," he said as if he was angry, but he held onto Gina's hand as if her hand was glued to his. Gina had never met such protective people before in her life. But she couldn't dwell on it. She was too worried about James.

But James had it well in hand. He stopped midway down the stairs and fired one shot just as Porterhouse Joe was about to run out of the front door. That shot was so close to Porterhouse that it singed his hair.

"I won't miss the second time!" James yelled. And Vincent, who was running down the stairs two at a time, was upon Porterhouse just as Porterhouse was raising his hands in surrender.

Vincent grabbed him and dropped him onto his stomach, his knee in the man's back.

Carmine, still holding Gina's hand, began running down the stairs with her as James made his way down to Porterhouse too.

"Turn his ass over," James ordered, his smoking gun still in his hand, and Vincent did just that. James was determined to get answers at last!

"I don't know what the fuck happened to my security," Carmine said. "I mean not one of those fuckers showed up. They allowed him to get into my house and all the way up to my bedroom. How the fuck did that happen? But I overpowered his ass and took his gun."

"They're dead, Carmine," Vincent said. "All of your security people were shot dead."

"What the fuck?" Carmine said, stunned. "I didn't hit a *got*damn shot. He had to have used silencers because I didn't hear shit."

"He did," James said as he pulled a semi-automatic handgun, with the silencer still on it, from out of Porterhouse's pocket. James opened the cylinder. It was empty. That was why it was in Porter's pocket.

Then James pointed his own gun at Porterhouse's face. "Why?" he asked him. "That's the only answer I want from you. Why?"

"I was in prison. Been there for seventeen years. But you knew that. You knew when I got locked up. We all were friends back then. But not one of yous came to visit me once."

"We looked out for your family," said Carmine. "What else could we do? You wasn't in our family. That shit you pulled had nothing to do with me. Your ass was just an acquaintance the way I saw it. But you asked me to look out for your old lady while you were away, and I did that."

"Vinny dated my daughter seventeen years ago," said Porterhouse.

Vinny frowned. "I didn't date your daughter. What daughter?"

"Penny Williams was my daughter!" Porterhouse yelled. "She had a different last name because her mother hated my guts, but she was my daughter. And you did date her. You dated through high school."

"Nobody knew she was your daughter," Vinny said.

But James, Gina could tell, looked distraught.

Then Porterhouse looked directly at James. "She was my daughter," he said, "and your ass killed her!"

Carmine frowned. "After she nearly killed our Vinny!" he yelled. "What the fuck you thought he was gonna do? Invite her over for fucking tea?! And Vinny's right. Nobody knew she was your daughter."

"That was fifteen years ago," Vinny said.

"Vinny was cheating on her," said Porterhouse. "She caught him with another woman at that pool party in Latham. That's why she shot him!"

Gina looked at James. She was floored. It was the same pool party where she and James had met. The night Tamira was conceived. It was the same night that Vincent was shot. She had no idea a girl had shot him. But it was the same night!

James knew it too, but he couldn't pull

himself to look at Gina. Not after she had to hear the truth about him. Not after she had to hear that he tracked down Penny Williams and shot her down like a dog in the streets. Vinny was on life support. She couldn't get away with what she'd done to him. But he had no idea Porterhouse Joe was her old man.

"When I found out you had a daughter, too," said Porterhouse, "I knew it was my chance then. We tried to run your ass down in that parking lot, but I hired an asshole who couldn't drive straight if his life depended on it. Then I found out, strictly by chance, that you had a daughter too. And I knew I could hurt you more by hurting her. She was supposed to die in that car crash, not that other girl. Merv was supposed to be the expert driver and see to that. But that's when I ordered my nephew to pay the other students in that car to point the finger at your kid. And they gladly did it. For the money."

Then Porterhouse smiled. "I just got out of prison couple months ago, now your daughter's in prison."

"Not for long," said James.

"You were the asshole I was hearing chatter about," Carmine said. "You were the one had a beef with Jimmy. But nobody was sure where the talk was coming from."

"It was coming from me," said

Porterhouse. "I even moved to Latham after I got out of prison, to be in the town where my daughter died. But while I was locked up, not a day went by when I wasn't plotting my revenge."

"Plot this, motherfucker," Carmine said, and shot Porterhouse in the shoulder.

Porterhouse screamed in agony, and so did James. "Carmine! Not until my daughter is free! We need his confession."

"We've got it," said Gina, and they all looked at her.

"What do you mean?" James asked.

"I pressed record on my cell phone when we came downstairs. I got him talking."

"You'll have to delete the part about Jimmy," said Vincent.

"I'll turn it over to James," she said. "I'll let him handle that."

Carmine smiled. "Good girl," he said, patting her hand. "You got a good, smart girl, Jimmy. Not like them buffoons you used to date."

James knew it, too, and he went over to Gina. But he had to pry Carmine's hand from hers before he could hug her. Then he hugged her. "Sorry you had to hear all of that," he whispered in her ear.

"Tamira will be free," said Gina happily. "We have something to give to that DA."

James couldn't agree more. But Carmine wasn't satisfied. He got down on his knees and pressed that gun against Porterhouse's neck. "You mention my brother or his girl and daughter, or any member of my family, and you're dead. You will make another recording where you admit setting Jimmy's girl up, and all that other shit you pulled, without mentioning any member of the Serrano family. Do I make myself clear? Because you've got other children around this world. You got other loved ones. I'll track each and every one of them down like dogs, but only after I take care of you."

Porterhouse knew Carmine was a nice guy, until he wasn't. When he wasn't, he was as vicious as they came. "I won't talk," he said. "I'll take my punishment. You won't have to harm any more of my family."

Carmine stood erect. James and Gina stood beside him. "Take him to the outhouse, Vinny. Record his confession. Use Gina's tape as backup. And then I'll call the commissioner to get a patrol car to pick him up anywhere except on my property."

"And your crew?" Vinny asked.

Carmine's jaws tightened. Wasn't much of a crew to have allowed a one-man ambush. "I'll call Bronson. He'll get a crew to handle the cleanup."

"I already called him. A crew is on the way," James said.

"Get up," said Vinny as he grabbed up the wounded Porterhouse, and took him to the study.

Then James looked at Carmine. And Carmine looked at James. They both knew, as soon as that confession was officially in the possession of the cops and Tamira was released, Porterhouse was dead meat. No way was he going to take out Carmine's entire security apparatus and live to tell the story. No way was he going to try and kill Tamira without retribution. No way was that happening, and James and Carmine both knew it.

"Take her home," Carmine said. "I'll get the evidence, and Porterhouse Joe, in the right hands. I want you and her completely hands off."

James looked at his brother. He started in the business as their old man's clean up man. "Always the cleanup man," James said. "Thanks, Carmine."

But Gina, so grateful she didn't know what to do, gave him a hug. He was a terrifying man in a lot of ways, but she was beginning to believe, when it came to family, that his bark was worse than his bite. "Thank you so much," she said, too.

Carmine smiled. His only hope was that she was as sweet as she seemed to be. "Now go," he said, and both James and Gina hurriedly left the scene.

But not before James teased her once they were outside. "Say, Bonnie, what you say we go get something to eat while we wait for Tamira's release?"

Gina smiled, immediately picking up on why he called her that name. "Sure thing, Clyde," she said, and they both laughed the laugh of two people finally happy and hopeful, and ready to begin again.

EPILOGUE

The door opened at Gina's house and James and Gina, with Tamira in front of them, walked in. As soon as Tamira entered, she opened her arms as if she were welcoming herself back home. "I miss my life so much!" she said.

Gina, shocked, looked at her and smiled. "You missed *this* life?"

"Yes! Don't look so shocked, Ma. Yes!"

"Okay. If you say so."

Then Kim, who was in the kitchen, came around the corner in an apron. "That you, Lil' Bit?" she asked, grinning.

When Tamira saw her, she ran to her. "Auntie Kim!" she cried, and they embraced vigorously.

But James gave Gina a hard look. And Gina understood his displeasure. "I talked to her," Gina said. "She knew she should not have mentioned anything about my private life to that so-called potential client. She knew she was wrong."

"And you still have confidence in her?" James asked her.

"Total," said Gina. "I don't know what I

would have done without Kim by my side all
these years. And just because she made one
big mistake, I can't throw her away. She's
staying by my side. Tamira and I are all she
has."

James stared at Gina. That was one of
the things he loved about her. She stood her
ground. She was willing to stand by a friend
despite what damage that friend could have
caused. "Then I have no issue with her, either.
But that could have gone all kinds of wrong."

Gina frowned and nodded her head. "It
truly could have. It went way wrong for Tonya."

James nodded to that. And then Kim and
Tamira stopped embracing. "Anyway, I know
you want to go and bathe all of that prison off of
you, so I'll be going."

"Going?" Tamira asked. "Why, Auntie?
Haven't you cooked dinner? Why won't you eat
with us?"

"Because," Kim said, "I have a hot date
for a change and I want to get myself together."

Gina knew Kim had no such date. She
was just afraid James was still pissed with her.
"I'll call you later, how about that?"

"Okay!" Tamira said with a smile, and
they hugged again.

Then Tamira ran back to her mother and
gave her a hug. And then she gave James a

hug, shocking James.

"Thanks, both of you, for getting me out of there," Tamira said.

James's heart melted. "You're welcome, Tamira," he said.

Tamira, satisfied that she'd done her bit, smiled. "I'll be in the tub, Ma," she said, and then hurried down the hall.

Kim began removing her apron. "There's still some fixings to prepare, and the meat's in the oven, but I'll get out of the way."

"You're staying for dinner, Kimmie," Gina said as she and James began walking over to her.

But Kim was shaking her head. "No, I've done enough damage thank you very much. I'll just---"

"You'll just what, Kim?" asked Gina. "Go home to your lonely apartment?" Gina shook her head. "No way. You're a part of this family, and you're staying with this family as we celebrate Tam's safe return."

Kim glanced at James. She knew he didn't want her there.

But James wasn't about to break up the relationship Gina and Tamira had with Kim, even though he disagreed vehemently with what she did. "We insist you stay," he said.

Kim was surprised, and her emotions

overtook her. Tears appeared in her eyes. "I never should have said a word to that man," she said. "Had I known who he was, I would have never---"

Gina put her arm around her. "We know, Kim. We know you would not have. We know, kiddo."

Kim wiped her tears away. "It'll never happen again," she promised.

"Oh, it had better not," Gina made clear, "or you'll be in the doghouse for good!"

Kim laughed. Gina and James smiled. "In that case," Kim said, "I'd better work for my meal. I'll finish dinner. It should be ready in thirty minutes or so."

"Sounds great," said James, and Kim, like Tamira, gave Gina a hug too. She wasn't comfortable enough with James to be that bold with him. And then she disappeared into the kitchen.

"Tam is going to be happy to see her at dinner," Gina said as she made her way over to the sofa.

"What about her hot date?" James asked as he followed her.

Gina smiled. Kim had about as much luck with men that Gina, before James, had been having. And she knew her hot date was going to be a lonely night alone. "I'm sure she'll have other opportunities."

James sat down beside her. She could tell how exhausted he was. "You know a lot of guys, don't you?"

"Yes," said James.

"Maybe you could find one suitable for Kim."

James thought about that. "I'll do my darndest," he said.

Gina smiled. "Thanks. Oh, and I forgot to ask."

"Ask what?"

"About the guy in the safe house. The one who tried to take you out in that parking lot. What became of him?"

James hated to discuss that part of his life. "He was taken care of," he said. "Vinny handled him."

Gina knew what that meant. "James?"

"Yes?"

"Are you in the Mafia?"

James hesitated. "Am I in it?" he asked. "No. Do I provide assistance to my brothers whenever they need it? Absolutely. Am I my brother's chief advisor? Yes. Yes, I am."

Gina exhaled.

"Do you think you're going to have a problem with that?" James asked her.

"You and I being officers of the court you

mean?" Gina asked.

"Yes," said James, staring at her.

But Gina was shaking her head. "You are who you are. I am who I am. I don't expect you to change for me. And I'm not going to change for you." Then she looked at him. "We'll work it out."

James smiled. He made the right choice. He could feel it in his bones. "I did it," he said.

Gina looked at him again. "You did what?"

"I approved your counteroffer in that factory case. Checks will be mailed out within five days," he added, "as per your request."

Gina was shocked. "Really, James?"

James folded his leg over his thigh. "It's the least I can do, Gina."

"The least? Are you kidding? You've done so much!"

"I haven't done a *got*damn thing. Not where it matters. Not concerning you. Not concerning Tamira." Then he looked at Gina. "When are we going to tell her?"

"Tell me what?"

When they heard Tamira's voice, they both nervously looked at her. She had returned to the living room. "I wasn't eavesdropping," she said. "They gave you my cell phone, Ma, and I came to ask you where you put it."

"It's in your desk drawer in your room," Gina said, staring nervously at Tam.

But Tamira would not be distracted. "Tell me what?" she asked them again.

James stood up. "Come sit beside your mother," he ordered her.

Tamira, staring at James the whole time, went and sat beside Gina. Gina placed her arm around her. She could feel Tamira already shaking, as if she thought it was going to be bad news. James sat on the coffee table in front of mother and daughter.

And Gina decided it was a story for her to tell. "I have something, "she started saying, and then caught herself. "*We* have something to tell you, Tam."

"What about?"

Gina swallowed hard. "About us. About you, and me . . . and Mister James."

"What about us?" Tamira asked, staring at her mother.

"You remember when I told you that your father. . . that your father was dead?"

Tamira hesitated. She looked so nervous to her parents that they weren't sure if she was anxious to hear the story, or dreaded hearing it. "Uh-hun," was all Tamira could manage to say.

Tears were already appearing in Gina's

eyes. "I told you that to protect you, so that you wouldn't feel abandoned. I told you that so that you wouldn't think any less of me than you already thought of me. I told you that because I might have been afraid that you would decide to search for him, and actually find him, and would leave me. Or worse, he would want to have nothing to do with you. I don't know all the reasons why I told you that, but . . . But what I told you wasn't true."

"What do you mean?" Tamira asked. "What wasn't true?"

"That your father was dead. That wasn't true."

Tamira's expression changed, but she didn't look surprised. "Ma, I been knew that," she said.

But Gina and James were surprised. Gina even removed her arm from around her daughter and turned toward her. "What do you mean you knew it?" she asked.

"I knew it," Tamira said. "I knew what you meant when you said he was dead."

Gina glanced at James, and then looked at Tamira again. "What do you think I meant?"

"I thought you meant he was dead to you. I thought you meant he had broken your heart or something, so he was dead to you and you didn't want to have anything to do with him. And since he broke your heart or hurt you in some way," Tamira said, looking over at James this time, "I didn't want to have anything to do with him either."

James's heart fell through his shoe. Gina was anguished as well. "But that's not true, baby," said Gina. "He didn't break my heart. He didn't hurt me in any way."

Tamira looked at her mother. "He didn't?"

"No," Gina said, shaking her head. "He didn't really know me, and I didn't really know him for either of us to do anything to each other."

Tamira stared at her mother. "You mean it was a booty call?" she asked her.

Gina would have thought they'd have a better name for it by now, but that was what it was. "Yes," she said. "It was a one-night-stand. And your father had no idea I was even pregnant. He had no idea you even existed or I'm certain he would have helped me raise you. But he didn't know you were on the face of this earth. And I didn't know how to find him either. Until now," Gina said.

When she said that, James knew it was his time to take the mantle of responsibility. "Your mother was very young when we got together, and she paid a steep price for that one-night-stand, including being kicked out of college."

Tamira looked at Gina. "You were kicked out of school just because you were pregnant?"

"It went against the rules of the school I attended, yes," said Tamira.

"Bayard?"

Gina nodded. "Yes."

"And she struggled," James continued, "and did all she could to find me. But that was my fault. I had given her the wrong name to begin with, and nobody in that town really knew me because I didn't live there. I was only in town to babysit my party-animal brother."

Tamira was staring at James. "What are you saying?" she asked him.

"I'm saying," James said, and then cleared his throat. "I'm saying that . . . I'm your father, Tamira. You're my child."

Gina and James both looked hard at Tamira to see just how she would react. Gina expected histrionics. James didn't know what to expect, but he suspected it would all be bad.

But Tamira surprised them both. She just nodded her head. "I figure as much," she said.

They both looked at her as if she was crazy. Gina was especially shocked. "How did you figure that, Tam?" she asked her.

"All of a sudden this man is doing all he can to help me," she said, "when you've never been with any man who gave me the time of day. Or you for that matter after they got what the wanted. But all of a sudden he's all interested in my welfare? And I know you couldn't afford to pay for an attorney. I already knew that. But to have a big-time attorney like him on my case? Even the guards told me he was a heavy hitter. I knew something was up. And when he came to see me at the detention center, and I saw him up close and personal beyond our first meeting at the hospital when I was too hysterical to see anybody, I knew he was my father."

"Just because he was nice to us?" Gina asked her.

"That," said Tamira, "and the fact that when I looked at him in that interview room at the detention center, I thought I was looking at myself. I saw me in him." Her eyes watered up. "I still do."

James stood up and grabbed her up and hugged her with a bear hug that almost squeezed the life out of her. And she hugged him back just as hard. James was in tears, and Gina was outright balling. She couldn't help it.

And then the doorbell rang, and none of them even heard it.

But Kim did. She came out of the kitchen shocked by what she was seeing, and then happy because she knew what it meant. They had told Tam! Tam now knew that James was her father. And Kim was elated too.

But the doorbell rang again, and she hurried and answered it.

"Yes? May I help you?"

James was the first to see his family at the front door. He and Tamira stopped embracing and Gina looked over there too. When she saw Carmine and Vincent at the front door with gifts in their hands, she stood up.

"What are you guys doing here?" James asked happily, wiping his tears away.

Kim stepped aside and Carmine and Vincent made their way inside. She closed the door behind them.

Carmine and Vincent were staring at Tamira. It was their first time seeing her. "We were in the neighborhood," Carmine said.

"*This* neighborhood?" asked Gina. "I don't think so!"

They laughed. "Okay, we weren't in the neighborhood," said Carmine, "but we wanted to wish the young lady a happy get out of jail," he said.

Tamira laughed. "That's funny," she said.

"It better be your first and last time," Carmine added. "Or you'll answer to me."

"Oh, it will be!" said Gina, and Tamira

smilingly rolled her eyes, which made Vincent laugh.

"Anyway," said James, "these two intruders are my brothers, Carmine and Vincent."

"Let me guess," said Tamira. "That's the party animal," she said, pointing at Vincent.

"Back in the day, my dear," said Vincent. "I'm a responsible adult now."

"He's an adult anyway," said Carmine. "I'm Carmine, by the way," he added, shaking Tamira's hand. "Nice to meet you," and then he caught himself. He almost called her his niece. But had they told her the truth? They had all been in tears, but that could have been from anything!

Until James made it clear. "Carmine, Vinny, this is Tamira. My daughter."

Carmine smiled. "So they told your ass, hun?" he asked Tamira.

Tamira grinned. She loved him already. "Yes, sir," she said.

"Then bring your ass over here," Carmine insisted, "and give your uncle a proper hug!"

Tamira moved closer to Carmine and he gave her a bear hug not unlike the squeezing kind James had given to her. "What's your last name again?" Carmine asked her when they stopped embracing.

"Griffin," Tamira said.

"Griffin my ass. You're a Serrano now. Tamira Serrano. That's you now."

Was this guy for real, Tamira wondered. Gina was laughing too. "Yes, sir," Tamira said.

"And James," Carmine said, "you had it all wrong. I don't see Vinny when I look at this beautiful specimen of a human being."

"I don't either," said Vincent. "I see James!"

"That's exactly who I see," said Carmine, but James nor Gina really saw the resemblance. Tam looked like Vincent to her, but she kept her mouth shut. She was just happy to be there.

They all settled down in the living room while Tamira went and took her bath. When she returned, and Kim announced that dinner was ready, Carmine and Vincent gave Tamira their gifts. Then Tamira and her parents, along with her uncles, all made their way to the dining room table.

But when Kim went to serve them, Gina stopped her. "No," she said. "I'll take over from here. You aren't the servant. You're family. Sit down with the family."

"Right next to me," Carmine said, patting the empty seat beside him. "You look like you could use a break."

"Oh, lord," said Vincent. "His mother hen is coming out again! Watch out, lady. Watch out!"

And they all laughed, and ate, and accepted each other for who they were.

Flaws and all.

Visit
www.mallorymonroebooks.com
or
www.austinbrookpublishing.com
or
www.teresamcclainwatson.com
for more information on all titles.

ABOUT THE AUTHOR

Mallory Monroe, a pseudonym of award-winning, bestselling literary author Teresa McClain-Watson, has well over a hundred bestselling books under her name.

Visit

mallorymonroebooks.com

or

austinbrookpublishing.com

or

teresamcclainwatson.com

for more information on all of her titles.

Made in the USA
Middletown, DE
05 November 2022

14197561R00201